Boss'N Up 2
The Naked Truth

Lock Down Publications
Presents
Boss'N Up 2
The Naked Truth
A Novel by *Royal Nicole*

LOCK DOWN PUBLICATIONS
PO BOX 870494
MESQUITE, TX 75187

VISIT OUR SITE WWW.LOCKDOWNPUBLICATIONS.COM

Copyright 2014 by Royal Nicole Boss'N Up 2

Lock Down Publications
Email: tha_raven08@yahoo.com
Facebook: Author Royal Nicole
Cover design and layout by: Dynasty's Cover Me
Book interior design by: Shawn Walker
Edited by: Mia Rucker

Royal Nicole

Chapter 1

The Naked Truth

"Don't move another step or I will splatter yo' shit all over this fucking floor," Zyon said while standing in place with his tool aimed at Ariel's pretty head ready to blast off. "Where is Yaseer?" he asked.

"Umm. Uh," Ariel started to lie but the blood on her clothes and the blade in her hand prevented that.

Zyon's eyes slowly traveled from her face down to the bloody weapon that she was clutching at her side. "Bitch, where the fuck is my brother?" he demanded.

She looked at him fearlessly. "Oh, that nigga is somewhere around here bleeding on the floor," she answered snidely.

Zyon studied her cold expression for a split second before the realization of what she was saying hit him square in the chest. His lip curled and his response was deadly. *Pow!* He let off one shot to her dome and watched her lifeless body drop. "Now so are you," he spat, walking past her corpse in search for his brother.

He almost walked past Yaseer's office until he noticed the door was ajar. He pushed the door open and saw Yaseer laid out on the floor with a pool of blood around him. "Help!" he screamed out, hoping that someone else was there to hear his pleas.

Yaseer was laid out on the floor dying all because he broke his number one rule: Never trust a bitch. After all the years of causing havoc in the streets, after all of the people he had killed young and old, the last thing he expected was to die from stab wounds that were inflicted by the mother of his children.

Of course, he knew eventually that bitch named Karma would catch up with him, but he thought he would at least go out getting wet up by the pigs, or some fools on some get-back type shit like a true G. Instead, there he was laid out on the floor at his warehouse bleeding out. He could hear muffled voices from afar. He heard his name being called and tried with all his might to respond before everything totally blacked out and death became the naked truth.

Paris was the first member of the crew to arrive at the sound of Zyon's pleas for help. She nearly fell out at the sight of her heart laid out on the floor with crimson fluid flowing out of his body. Her breath hitched before she let out a scream that would have put a wild banshee to shame as she fell to her knees beside Yaseer.

"Nooooo! You can't leave me, Yaseer. Noooo!"

Liam, Kai'Yan, and London filed into the room as soon as the frantic words escaped Paris' mouth. For a split second, their world came to a standstill before everyone jumped into action.

"What the fuck happened, Zy?" Liam questioned his older brother as he grabbed ahold of Paris and ushered her over to where London stood in shock.

"I'll explain shit later. Right now, we got to get him to the hospital and somebody gotta clean up that bitch's thoughts that I just put on public display."

"What bitch?" London asked in a deadly quiet voice.

"London, I will answer all that shit later. We have to go!" Zyon yelled impatiently.

"Help me lift him up and get him to the car, Liam. Kai'yan, handle everything else," Zyon spat.

Liam sprang into action. He grabbed Yaseer's legs while Zyon had his forearms, supporting Yaseer's upper body as they carried him to Zyon's blacked-out Navigator.

Tears flowed from Paris' eyes as they rode in the car with London in complete silence. The only noise in the car was the lyrics of August Alsina's song *Kissin' on My Tattoo's* crooning softly through the speakers. The mere thought of losing Yaseer had her entire being shattered into a million and one pieces. Life without him would be equal to her being six feet under.

Paris' mind flashed back over the past year. She saw herself getting out of prison after taking a gun charge for Yaseer, finding out about his infidelities, the whole situation with Ezra, the rape, getting shot, Brooklyn being shot, and finally being able to get revenge only to turn around and have Yaseer at the brink of death. Paris' tear flow increased and she began to choke on her sobs. She was almost to the point of hyperventilation.

"Paris, you have to pull yourself together. Sis, we got to think positive. My future brother-in-law will be just fine. You will see."

"But, but what if…" Paris began, but couldn't even bring herself to formulate the words *dead and Yaseer* in the same sentence.

"No what if's. Now pull yourself together, put on your Boss hat, and let's go watch these doctors save his life," London said as they pulled up to the hospital.

Zyon and Liam were already there. Paris was determined to ride in the car with Yaseer but Zyon quickly vetoed that idea by telling her she didn't need to be on the radar when police came asking the five W's. Paris knew he was right, being that she had just got out of prison, so she agreed to ride with her sister.

Paris stepped out of the car, wiped her tear-stained face, and tried to fix herself before she entered the doors of the hospital. Sure her heart was in a ruckus, but at the moment she needed to be a boss so she could talk to the doctors in the hospital like she had some sense. She couldn't do that if she was crying and her words were barely audible.

A Few Hours later...

Paris' head popped up at the sound of the doctor's voice.

"Is this the Davis family?" he questioned.

"Yes it is," Paris answered as she rushed to stand to her feet and approach the doctor. As soon as she took her first step, a wave of dizziness hit her and nearly knocked her off of her feet.

"Paris!" Liam exclaimed as he grabbed her to keep her from falling.

"Ma'am, are you okay?" Dr. Barnett asked as he stepped over to where Liam had Paris embraced in his arms, making sure she had her balance.

"Yes, I'm okay. I just got real dizzy for a moment."

"How often are you having these dizzy spells?"

"I have only had them a few other times in the last few weeks. I'm okay though. How is my fiancé? Will he be

9

okay?" Paris asked with concern etched all over her face. Dr. Barnette held his breath for a moment and then answered the question that everyone was dying to know the answer to.

"We were able to stop the bleeding. However, due to the extent of his injuries, he has fallen into a coma. He will live, but we do not know when he will come of out of it. Only time will tell," the doctor concluded.

Paris stood there in a daze. She was beyond excited that her heart would live, but was down because she didn't know when she would hear his voice again or be able to look in his beautiful chocolate orbs again. That was fucking with her to the fifth degree.

Chapter 2

Welcome Home

Three Months Later…

"Ooh, bae, these children of yours is kicking my ass for real, for real," Paris said as she brushed Yaseer's hair, which had grown out into a shoulder-length curly mane.

"I can't wait to give birth to these big babies. You should see how fat I'm getting," Paris stated as she continued grooming Yaseer. He had yet to come out of his coma and Paris was hoping he would be there to witness the birth of their unborn children.

"I already have their names picked out. I hope you like them, bae. I was thinking about you when I picked them out."

Paris stared down into the handsome face of her fiancé and silently wished for him to awaken. She missed him so much and longed to hear his voice, feel his touch, and the caress of his lips on hers. God how she missed the love of her life.

"Well, babe, I got a doctor's appointment to go to. I'll be back, love," Paris said as she leaned over and gave him a kiss on his soft lips and then turned to exit the hospital room.

"Ppp—Paris," Yaseer stuttered in a voice just above a whisper.

Paris stopped in her tracks. Her ears had to be deceiving her. She shook her head and reached for the door to exit the room.

"Paris," Yaseer called out in a little stronger voice.

Paris paused. She knew as sure as she knew her name was Paris that she was not going insane. She slowly turned around, praying that what she dreamed of day and night had finally come true. She looked over at a drowsy Yaseer whose eyelids were low but open enough that she could look into his eyes.

Paris' heart sped up and her feet took off.

"Baaabeee! Oh, my—Oh, my God, you're awake. You're awake," Paris screamed as she ran to his bedside and engulfed him in an embrace.

A nurse, who happened to be passing by the room door, heard the scream and ran in thinking someone was in trouble. When she walked in and saw Yaseer awake, she ran back out to call for assistance. Normally, she would have been assigned to him on the days she worked, but that day was supposed to be her day off. She was only there helping out because a nurse had a family emergency and had to leave early. Seeing him awake had her beyond excited. She prayed that the lord would give this young man another chance. She didn't know exactly what happened to land him in this predicament, but she hoped that he would never have to endure this again. Other nurses and the on-call doctor came running into the room to get vitals on Yaseer and check him out. Paris was pushed to the side as they looked him over.

A week later, Yaseer was released to go home. Yaseer was beyond agitated because he couldn't get used to being in a wheelchair, but that was how life would be for a while due to his temporary paralysis. However, he was more than happy to be going home with the love of his life, whom he had just found out was expecting a set of twin boys. He was over the moon happy about that.

"Welcome home!" TTC greeted from the foyer as Yaseer rolled into his house with Paris behind him.

"What the hell?" Yaseer mumbled trying to conceal his grin. He had one of the best families and he knew it. The love they had for one another was unconditional and untouchable.

"What up, boy?" Zyon spoke as he dapped his brother up, followed by Kai'yan, Liam, and Brooklyn.

"Nun much, bruh, just tryna hang in here, tryna get use to this wheelchair shit."

"I feel you, bro, and don't worry we will help you

adjust as much as we can. Follow me in the dining room," Zyon spat as he turned and headed into the kitchen with the crew in tow.

Yaseer rolled into the dining room and was touched by the gesture everyone had made on his behalf. There, in the middle of the table, sat a large cake that read: Welcome Home. Alongside it were gifts and plentiful food. This would be a day he would never forget but he refused to be the only one acknowledged, knowing there had been other victims besides himself.

"Come 'ere, Brooklyn and Paris." They both made their way over to where Yaseer sat in his wheelchair beside the table.

"What you want, big head?" Brooklyn teased.

"Yo Iraqi looking ass always got jokes," Yaseer joked before getting serious.

"I appreciate everything you all have done for me and the crew. Paris, you stuck by me even after my infidelities caused you to leave me and end up getting hurt by Ezra. For that I am grateful and truly sorry for all the pain you endured. Brooklyn, you are out here risking your life and even took a bullet that almost cost you your life because you want to hold us down as a family unit. I am beyond grateful for you as well. This celebration is for all of us making it to see another

14

day, even when things looked bleak. Now with that being said, I love y'all but I'm ready to eat something other than that damn hospital food," Yaseer concluded with a smirk on his face. They laughed, joked, and ate until around 10pm before everyone started leaving slowly but surely.

"Aye, Liam, can you give London a ride home? Me and Brooklyn got something we need to handle before we go home," Kai'yan asked.

Liam looked at Kai'yan like he had just grown two heads, but quickly dismissed the expression, not wanting to get London riled up. "Yea, I got you, fam."

"I know you do," Kai'yan responded over his shoulder as he and Brooklyn said their goodbyes and left.

Liam went back into the living room in search of London so they could leave only to find a sleeping London balled up in the corner of the black sectional couch. He stood there for a moment and just gazed at her. *Damn, she is beautiful*, he thought to himself. His green orbs trailed London from the top of her head to her beautiful almond shaped eyes, her pert nose, plush pink lips, to the curls that flowed past her shoulders onto her perky breasts, down to the expand of her hips that gave way to a luscious round ass. His dick jumped just looking at her. Liam inhaled a breath and held it. He had to control his feelings. It was not the time for his soldier to salute the world.

"Damn," Liam mumbled under his breath as he adjusted himself before walking over to London. He gently tapped her on the shoulder to tell her it was time to go and that she would be riding with him instead of Kai'yan and Brooklyn, who she had originally rode with over to her sister's place.

"London, London," Liam called out in a low voice as he tapped her shoulder again. London opened her eyes slowly and peered up at him through sleepy eyes. For a hint of a second, their gazes held before Liam spoke.

"You ready to go?" he asked.

"Yeah, let me grab my purse. Tell Brooklyn I'm coming," London answered in a sleep filled voice.

"About that, they had to leave to go take care of a few things and asked if I could drive you home. So, you riding with me, ma."

That one statement woke London all the way up. "Oh, okay I guess," London responded. Liam started to say something smart but bit his tongue. He was not in a mood to argue so he just let her ungratefulness slide.

Chapter 3

Why?

London got into Liam's car thinking. *Why the hell did I listen to Brooklyn and car pool with her? Now I am stuck in the car with him.* It wasn't that she didn't like Liam. The problem was that she liked him a little too much. Just being around him had her kitty ready to be fed his creamy substance. She rested her head on the headrest and closed her eyes to avoid having to see him.

Liam turned the music on softly. DJ Khaled's song *I Wanna Be with You* was playing softly throughout the car.

Ballin' on you too easy/ Splurging on you too easy/ Buying cars too easy/ Popping bottles too easy/ I wanna be with you/ I wanna be with you/ Everything you do is brand new...

Liam bobbed his head to the lyrics. The lyrics were really fucking with him, but he wasn't the only one being affected by the words coming through the speakers. London could have sworn the lyrics were speaking to her.

You decide you be mine/ You can come inside/ You the type that can make me prioritize/ Hittin' my phone is alright/ Hittin' my phone is alright.

If London didn't know any better, she would have

thought Liam played that song on purpose. They both remained silent through the entire ride. Liam pulled into the driveway to London's house, put the car into park, and shut off the ignition. London pressed the unlock button and made a move to get out of the car. Liam pressed the lock button on his side and relocked the doors. She looked over her shoulder with a mug on her face that would have put Ice Cube's mean mug to shame.

"Why, London?"

"Why what? Liam, let me out the damn car."

"Why do you always got to be so damn mean? What gets me is that you always aim your smart remarks and shit my way. Have I offended you in anyway unknowingly? 'Cause if so, I will be glad to offer you an apology."

London took a deep breath before responding to him. "Liam it's not you, it's me."

"Really London, could you be anymore more original than that?" Liam said as he shook his head.

"Well, it is me. You wouldn't understand."

"How do you know that I wouldn't understand? You'll never know if I will understand or not if you don't try to break it down to me," Liam spat back.

"Okay, you wanna keep barking up this tree so I will damn sure break it down to you like a fuckin' fraction,"

18

London said. She turned her body in the seat, leaned over, and got all up in Liam's grill, stopping a breath away from his face.

"You really wanna know why I always got something smart to say to you and only you? You really want to know why I don't like to be in your presence? Do you really wanna know why you wouldn't understand that it's me who has the problem and it's not because of anything you did intentionally?" London spat barely above a whisper.

"Yea, I do," Liam answered in a soft voice. London grabbed Liam's free hand and guided it between the apexes of her legs, then stuck the tip of her tongue out and licked his full lips.

"You see that Liam? You feel how wet my pussy get from just being in your presence?" She whispered in his ear. She swirled her tongue in a circle on the side of his neck before bringing her lips back to his ear. "That's why I can't stand to be around you. I can't stand how my body loses control any time you walk into a room, anytime you say something, any time you look at me, knowing ain't shit I can do to fulfill that need. My battery operated boyfriend couldn't even fix the problem for me. That is why I said it's not you it's me. Is that original enough for you, baby?" London questioned before she unlocked the doors, got out of the car, and trotted up to her humble abode.

Liam sat there in shock, trying to gather his thoughts. He couldn't believe what had just happened. He licked his lips and could taste the strawberry lip gloss that was on her lips.

Liam unbuckled his seatbelt and jumped out of his black 2014 Chrysler 200. If she thought he was about to let her slide with that shit then she must have truly lost her mind.

Knock! Knock! Knock! Liam banged on London's door.

London opened the door with an attitude, not wanting to deal with him at the moment.

"What—" she didn't even have time to fully respond before Liam grabbed ahold of her waist, pulled her to him, and then brought his lips down to hers. It all happened so fast that London didn't even have time to protest.

Liam backed London up through the open door and used his foot to close it. He backed her up into a wall, trapping her in between him and the wall. Liam let his hands caress her ass before bringing them down to her thick thighs, grabbing ahold of them, and picking her up. London wrapped her long shapely legs around his waist. He began to slowly grind his middle between her thighs.

Damn, she feels so good, Liam thought to himself. His

20

body was on fire and she was the only one who could extinguish it.

"You know how long I been longing for you, ma?" Liam whispered on her wet lips. "Longing for your body, your touch, your kiss. Longing to know how it would feel to slide deep up in your saturated walls. I think about you day and night, wondering what if. Do you know how long I've been longing to capture your heart and make you mine?" Liam questioned, and then kissed her lips softly before pulling back just a hair to speak to her. "I want you, London. I need you, ma."

London brought her hand to the back of Liam's head and pulled his lips to hers. Liam used his tongue to explore places in London's mouth that no other man had even come close to. London pulled his bottom lip in between her teeth gently before letting her tongue out to play with its mate.

Liam carried London down the hall to her bedroom, pushed the door open, and then proceeded to lay her down on her California King. He intensified their kiss as he continued his slow grind between her legs.

Chapter 4

New Flame

London's hands trailed their way to the hem of Liam's shirt and pushed it up, revealing his caramel six pack. London's pussy dripped just looking at that much of his flesh. She pushed the shirt over his head and marveled at the art work on his left peck and shoulder. She ran her hands over his tattoos as she looked him in the eyes. This was what she wanted. There were many nights she pleasured herself as she fantasized about having him buried to the hilt inside of her. Now, her dream was finally becoming reality and she could hardly wait for the real thing.

Liam stared at the angel that lay sprawled out in front of him. His dick was stone hard. He was determined that by the time he was done with her tonight, he would have left his mark like he was leaving the mark of the beast. Liam brought his lips to London's and kissed her with all the passion he had built up in him. He slowly pulled away from her lips and let his kisses fall to the side of her neck on down to her collarbone and then back up to her neck. He used his tongue to put his signature on her neck, using his saliva to mark his territory.

Liam slid down his counterpart's body until he was face to face with the button of her jeans. He unbuttoned the button, unzipped them, and slid them down her thick silky thighs. There before him was his feast, staring him in his face through the fabric of a black laced thong.

Liam grabbed the sides of the thin material and ripped them clean off of her body. He was always taught not to play with his food and tonight would be no different. Liam stuck the tip of his tongue out and swiped it slowly down her dripping center. She had one of the most beautiful pussies he had ever seen. He separated her folds with his fingers and penetrated her using his tongue. His tongue imitated what his manhood would be doing soon.

Liam sucked her womanly folds in between his lips. He pulled the hood of clitoris back and flicked his tongue in a rapid pace before sucking it into his mouth. Liam released her clit and started kissing his way back up her body. He put his hands under her camisole and pushed it over her head. Then he unclasped her bra in the front and removed that as well.

Liam stood up and removed his dark blue True Religion jeans, along with his boxers, wheat Timbs, and socks. Liam stood before London in all his glory, ready to make love to the woman who had clouded his thoughts day and night. Liam climbed in between London's parted thighs with his piece aimed at London's womanhood. He leaned down and kissed her seductively.

The thought of condoms crossed his mind. But he had waited for so long for the opportunity to feel her insides that when he did, he didn't want any barriers. He wanted to feel her, all of her. Liam began to push the massive head of his steel inside of her and then pulled back. Again, he repeated the process and found it a little hard to get inside of her tight, moist kitty.

Liam looked down at London with a befuddled look on his face. *No,* he thought to himself. He ceased all movement and locked his gaze on London's beautiful chocolate orbs.

"Lon—" She placed her delicate index finger on his lips to halt the question he was about to ask. She just simply nodded her head *yes*.

"Don't stop," she said breathlessly. Liam was in awe of what he had just found out. It took his heart by storm that she was trusting him with the precious gift of her virginity. He would be her first and if things went his way, he would be her one and only, her last. Liam repeated the process again, this time easing in a little more. He pulled back a little and eased in some more until he got past the barrier that was blocking his entrance.

24

"Shit," Liam mumbled under his breath. The feeling of her insides wrapped around his member like a glove had him mesmerized.

London moaned out in pain and pleasure at the intrusion that was feeling better and better with each stroke taking any memory of the pain that was just caused moments before away. He began to move in and out of her body slowly. Looking into her eyes as he made love to her, Liam felt his heart expand. All of the love he had for her that had built up over time was coming to a head. Never in his life had he felt this way for any female. He didn't understand it and didn't want to. It was just something about her that drove his emotions wild. He had her now and it was no way in hell he was letting her go. Liam rotated his hips in a circular motion, making sure he hit every nook and crevice.

"Oh, shit. Harder, Liam, harder," London moaned out as she dug her manicured nails into his back.

Liam ignored the pain from her nails. Hearing her moan out his name made his dick harder. Liam dipped down as he went in and started long dicking the hell out of London. He placed one of her legs in the crook of his arm and started going deeper and faster. He gritted his teeth together. He was trying his best not to cum early but the way her slippery walls were milking him had him ready to shoot his load deep inside of her.

"Damn, ma, you feel so good," Liam muttered under his breath.

"Liam, fuck me. Fuck me harder, daddy."

"This my pussy. You hear me?" Liam said in between pumps.

"Yes! Yes!" London moaned out.

"Don't you give my shit to no one else, you hear me?" Liam hissed as he gripped her hips and pumped harder.

"Yaasss."

"Whose pussy is this?"

"Yours," London moaned out.

"Whose?"

"Yours."

"What's my name?"

"Liam," London screamed out in sheer ecstasy.

Hearing London scream his name, combined with her womanly folds clenching his manhood, caused him to shoot his seed deep in her womb. He didn't even think twice about letting off inside of her. If she was on birth control, then cool. And if she wasn't, it was still fine with him. He was a man. He knew how to take care of his business. He had plenty of money so he didn't even fret at the possibility of having to take care of another life. In his mind, London now belonged to him and he was determined to keep it that way. She was who he wanted and that was that. He fell in love with her as soon as he laid eyes on her. He felt it love at first sight. And tonight was their beginning together. It was something new that they both would have to get used to.

Chapter 5

Adjusting

"Damn, I gotta get used to this shit," Yaseer mumbled to himself as he rolled himself into the kitchen. He was hungry as shit and had to find something to eat on until Paris woke up to cook. She was sleeping so peacefully that he didn't want to disturb her. She had helped him out a lot the previous night. She washed him off and helped him transfer into the bed using the methods the staff at the hospital had shown her. So he was more than willing to let her catch some extra Z's.

Yaseer opened the refrigerator and sat there debating what he wanted to snack on. He chose a container of assorted fruits and a bottle of Sprite to munch and sip on until Paris woke up. Yaseer put the fruit and bottle of soda on his lap and started making his way out of the kitchen, but stopped to pick up a bag of ranch Doritos on the counter to add to his snack collection.

Yaseer rolled into the living room, placed his snacks on the end table beside the couch, then picked up the remote off of the table in the center of it, and turned on his sixty-five-inch TV that was mounted on the wall. He pressed the On Demand button, went to Starz, and turned on his favorite show by 50 Cent called Power.

Yaseer loved how the show portrayed the life he actually led. He also liked how the main character was trying to get away from the drug life because deep down that was something he longed for. He knew a drug dealer's lifespan wasn't long. He also knew selling drugs could get his loved ones hurt when jealousy and greed came into the mix. He was far from ready for those consequences. He had come close enough to losing his sister and fiancé due to envy, which was a feeling he never wanted to feel again.

Yaseer's head snapped toward the entrance of the living room when he heard footsteps. A huge smile came across his face when he saw his baby walk in the room.

Paris walked into the living room to see a smiling Yaseer sitting in front of the TV watching her as she came in. Paris walked over, leaned down, and gave him what was supposed to be a peck but, as usual, it became more than a peck.

Yaseer held the side of Paris face with his right hand as his left hand found its way to the ample roundness of her backside. Yaseer deepened the kiss as his hand continued its exploration of her body. His hand found its way to the waistband of the black boy shorts she was wearing. He dropped the hand that was holding on to the side of her face

29

to the other side of her waistband. Yaseer slid the boy shorts down her thick thighs, only to come face to face with plump mound.

Paris stepped out of her shorts as Yaseer pulled her by her hips to bring her mid-section closer to his face. Yaseer looked up at her face from his seated position. Then he let his gaze travel the length of her thick body. He licked his lips in anticipation of the meal he was about to get fed.

"Put yo leg up here, ma," he said as he nodded his head in the direction of the armrest opposite the one she stood in front of.

Paris complied with his request.

Yaseer grabbed ahold of her ass and brought his hungry mouth to Paris' dripping center. Paris placed her hand on the back of Yaseer's head as she let her head fall back while she enjoyed the sweet torture of Yaseer's tongue.

"Oh… shit, Yaseer," Paris moaned out. She thrust her hips forward in a sensual manner. Yaseer gripped her flesh tighter to hold her in place while he ate from the buffet that was displayed in front of him.

"Yaass! Yassss! Mhmm! Yaaseeer!" Paris hissed out in between heavy breaths as her core began to reach its boiling point. She held on to Yaseer's head tighter, making sure that he stayed in place.

Yaseer removed a hand from her plump ass and inserted his index and middle fingers deep inside of Paris' canal. He moved them in and out of her tight kitty. He paused his hand movement for a brief second, only to add his ring finger to the mix. He eased his fingers back inside of Paris' wet walls, and then began to pump them in and out like he would do with his manhood. Yaseer sought out that rigid spot and when he found it, he let his fingers go to work while the tip of his tongue put in overtime on her clit.

"Fuck! Ugghh!" Paris moaned out.

Yaseer felt her walls began to contract around his fingers. He removed them, filled the spot his fingers had vacated with his tongue, and let it finish up the job. Paris' juices squirted in Yaseer's mouth. He made sure not to let any juices escape. He had eaten a good meal and now he was thirsty. Thanks to his baby, his thirst was being well quenched.

Paris' body jerked a little with aftershocks of her orgasm before settling down. Paris dropped her leg back down to the floor. She pulled Yaseer's head to her belly, bent over slightly, and kissed the top of Yaseer's head. Then she rested her cheek on the top of his head as she waited for her breathing to return to normal.

"I love you, Paris, don't you ever forget that."

"I love you too, Seer. Ya hungry, bae?" Paris asked.

Yaseer lifted his head and looked at her with a serious expression. "I just ate a full course meal," he said as a smirk appeared on his face.

Paris started laughing and mushed his head. "Smart ass, I'm talking about real food."

"Pussy is real food. Ask the Asian's."

"You need ya ass whooped. Alright Kevin Hart, don't be crying you hungry later on. By the way, how did you get in your chair?"

A gloomy look passed over Yaseer's face before he responded. "I rolled out of bed onto the floor and used my elbows to crawl to my chair. Once I got there, I made sure the wheels were locked, grabbed on to the arms of the chair, pulled up til' my waist was at the edge of the seat, turned around, and sat down. Then voila, I was in my chair," Yaseer announced with a shrug of his shoulders as if it was nothing. Even though it was a challenge for him to get to and in his chair by himself, he was determined to not be needy. He had always done for himself and that wasn't about to change because he was bound to a chair.

A frown came over Paris' beautiful face before she questioned Yaseer. "Why didn't you wake me up so I could have helped you?"

"Because I didn't need your damn help," Yaseer spat

with attitude laced through his words.

Paris leaned back, looked at him like he had just grown a third eye, and then scrunched her top lip up in a scowl. "You know what? You sure didn't, did you? So when you hungry, need a bath, or ready to get in the bed, remember you don't need my help," Paris said in a quiet voice. Then she bent down, picked her shorts up, put them on, turned around, and exited the room the same way she had come in.

"Paris—Paris!" Yaseer yelled out as he rolled out of the living room chasing after her.

"Paris, I didn't mean to snap like that. I'm sorry," Yaseer continued ranting as he continued in search for his other half. Just as he got to their bedroom he saw Paris coming out of the room dressed in some black sweats, a wife beater, with some 23's on her feet and Michael Kors pocketbook in tow.

"Where you going, P?"

"To the store, Yaseer. Damn, I don't need you questioning me just like you didn't need my help," Paris hissed as she maneuvered to walk past Yaseer. He grabbed her by her arm as she attempted to pass by him. He pulled her backwards and tugged her down on his lap.

"Bae, I'm sorry, I didn't mean to get slick wit you like that. This paralyzed shit is getting to me, ma. This

33

wheelchair stuff is taking me some time to adjust to. You know I'm used to being up and about handling business. I apologize, you know me better than that. You know I ain't mean to go in on you like that."

"I understand that, but you can't take how you feel out on me. We can talk about your feelings, but you not about to yell them at me or take your frustrations out on me. I'm almost five months pregnant and don't need the stress. So next time, either talk to me about your feelings or swallow them words back down ya throat. Clear?"

"Yeah, I hear ya, ma. Hold on, did you just handle me like my name was Raggedy Ann?"

"Only yo ass would say something so stupid," Paris said with a smile as she made a movement to get up off of Yaseer's lap. He tightened his grip on Paris.

"What you 'bout to go get from the store, ma? The cabinets and fridge are stocked up for the month already."

"I'm craving some fried Oreo's and we don't have any more Oreos left for me to make some. You ate the last of them last night."

"They was good as hell, too," Yaseer replied with a snicker. "Alright, you got dem tools wit ya?"

"Yeah, I got 'em. You know I ain't going nowhere without my twin nines."

34

"This I know," Yaseer responded as he let Paris off of his lap. "Aye bae, bring me back a banana pudding milkshake from the Cookout on ya way back."

"Got ya. Anything else, my King?" Paris questioned just as she reached the door.

"Oh yeah, bring me some Gummy Worms," he yelled toward the door.

"K," Paris yelled back. Then she walked out the door to go make her runs so she could get back before the Law & Order: SVU marathon started.

Chapter 6

Future

"Get 'em, Elliott," Brooklyn screamed at the TV.

"B, you act like they can hear you," Kai'yan spat over her shoulder.

"I know that, but you know I go cray over my Law & Order: SVU, CSI, and Scandal. All other life forms around me are non-existent when they on."

"Don't I know it, but you forgot there is always one thing existent even when you on fantasy island," Kai'yan replied as he used the hand he had draped across her waist to pull her backside closer to his body.

"And what's that?" Brooklyn asked softly as she looked back at him. Her eyes dropped from his eye's to his lips.

"This." Kai'yan kissed her on her neck. "This," he said, and then gave her a peck on her lips. "This," he spat as his hand trailed in front of her to the inside of her panties. "And this," Kai'yan whispered as he ground his hips against Brooklyn's full ass.

Brooklyn moaned out in pleasure. Kai'yan was right about that. She could never resist his touch, even in dreamland. She turned over from the side she was laying on onto her back and wrapped her arms around his neck. Kai'yan climbed in between her thick thighs and looked her in her chocolate orbs, silently expressing his love for her. He flung his shoulder blade length dreads out of his face, and then bent down and kissed Brooklyn with all the love in his heart. He held himself up above her with one hand while he used his other to pull his basketball shorts down. Then he pulled Brooklyn's panties down her thighs. He continued kissing Brooklyn as he eased the massive head of his dick inside of Brooklyn's womanhood. Brooklyn's back arched off of the bed at the pleasure of his entry.

Kai'yan moved gently making sure not to cause her any pain. Kai'yan's lips trailed down to the side of her neck. He stuck out the tip of his tongue to let it taste test the sweetness of Brooklyn's skin. A moan escaped her plush lips at the wonderful sensations Kai'Yan was bestowing upon her. Kai'yan leaned his hips slightly to the side so that he could massage her insides at an angle. He wanted to make sure he didn't miss a spot.

Brooklyn's petite hands came from around Kai'yan's neck to his shoulder blades. She pushed against his shoulders to indicate to him to get off of her. He paused his movement and looked at her to make sure she was okay. Before he could let the question escape his mouth, Brooklyn answered it knowing he would be worried about her and their unborn seed.

"I'm okay. Flip over, I wanna ride."

A smirk came across Kai'yan's lips in the dark room only illuminated by the light of the TV. Kai'yan climbed from between Brooklyn's legs and lay in the position that his woman wanted him in. Brooklyn pulled her spaghetti strapped shirt over her head. Her perky breasts stared directly at Kai'yan's lustful gaze. He placed his hands on her sides as she climbed on top of him onto his tool. He held her waist as she slid down on his stick. The erotic sight of his pregnant woman on top of him made his dick harden even more. The sight was so beautiful to him.

Brooklyn winded her hips back and forth, up and down. The image looked like a belly dancer riding a horse. Kai'yan sat up while she continued to ride his tool like she was a top notch paid porn star. He wrapped his arms around her back and pulled her breasts to his bare chest. He brought his hand up to the back of Brooklyn's head, gripped a handful of her silky strands, and tugged her head back so that he could get a good view of her neck.

Kai'yan's lips found his favorite spot on her neck and he French kissed it like he would kiss her lips. He sucked her

38

soft skin in between his lips making sure to leave his mark. Brooklyn rode him harder. Moans filled the atmosphere as the two made love. Kai'Yan pulled her as close to his chest as her abdomen would allow and he held on tight as his seed shot up in her womb.

The feeling of his release triggered Brooklyn's release. She screamed out his name in ecstasy. She rested her forehead on his forehead as her movements slowed to a smooth stop.

"I'ma kick yo ass," she said in between pants.

Kai'yan gave her lips a peck as a smile came over his face. "What I do?" Kai'yan feigned innocence.

"You knew soon as you touched me Law & Order was a wrap. Now I done missed the rest of that episode and the beginning of the next," Brooklyn pouted.

"Well it ain't my fault you can't resist the D," Kai'yan cracked.

"Shut up," Brooklyn spat as she burst into laughter, got off of Kai'yan, and snuggled up beside him. Kai'yan wrapped his muscular arm around Brooklyn's waste.

"I love you, Kai."

"I love you, too, love," he responded along with a kiss on her forehead.

"I am so happy things are getting back to normal,

bae," Brooklyn said in a soft voice.

"Me too, bae, it feels good to kick back again without the drama or having to watch our backs."

"Say that again, we finally get to relax. We should take a vacation, bae."

"You know what? That's actually not a bad idea. Where you wanna go?"

Brooklyn pondered the question for a moment before responding.

"Let's go to Cabo San Lucas," she replied, feeling giddy at the possibility of going on a vacation and being able to relax before it was time to get back to the hustle.

"When you wanna leave?"

"Let's leave a week exactly from today."

"Okay cool, next Friday it is," Kai'yan obliged.

Nothing could ruin the feeling they were feeling at the moment. Yaseer had pulled through his near death experience, as well as Brooklyn. Everyone was healthy and they were officially done with having to worry about anyone plotting to snuff their lives out. Or so he thought.

Chapter 7

Unexpected

A week had passed since Yaseer and Paris had their mini falling out after he somewhat lost his temper with her. Now things were going smoothly and he was getting stronger and stronger every day. Twice a day, Yaseer had a therapist come to work with him so he could walk again. He was making great progress. Determination is a beast when you really want something and Yaseer really wanted to walk again. He was determined that he would do so sooner rather than later.

Yaseer had just finished up a phone call with his connect. It was getting close to time for them to re-up on their supply. He was on his way to his version of a man cave when he heard his doorbell ring. Yaseer pulled his tool off of his ankle and placed it on his lap. He wasn't expecting company and Paris had a key so he was curious as to who was at his door.

"Who is it?" Yaseer questioned with a bass filled voiced. No one responded.

"Who is it?" Yaseer asked once more. Again, no response.

Yaseer's curiosity was now peaked at who had the

41

audacity to ring his doorbell but didn't have balls enough to respond. Yaseer yanked the door open with his tool aimed. The only thing he saw was the tail lights of some coward's car. He almost shut the door back when he heard a squeal and looked down, only to see his twin baby girls at his doorstep along with their baby bags.

Yaseer's heart broke. With everything going on with him just waking up out of a coma and all, he had forgotten all about his baby girls. He hadn't even asked about Ariel. He assumed that she had gotten away and gotten the hell out of dodge. Now his head was full of questions. His main question was where was she? He needed to find her so he could serve her a fate much worse than what she had done to him, and worse than she could ever think of. Yaseer was also mad at himself for not remembering to ask about his children. That was something that would be hard for him to ever forget.

Yaseer put the lock back on his gun, placed it in its ankle holster, and then bent over as far as he could in his chair without flipping over. He grabbed ahold of the handle on Chaunte's car seat, picked it up, and placed it on his lap. He rolled backwards just a little while keeping his eyes trained on Madison. He placed Chaunte on the floor beside him, and then rolled back to the door and mimicked what he had done with Chaunte with Madison. Then he rolled back to the door and picked up their baby bags, placed them on his lap, rolled backwards, and closed and locked the door.

Then he rolled over to where his daughters sat in their car seats. He looked at their beautiful faces for a brief moment before realizing how hard it was going to be to take care of them in his predicament. Hell, he needed someone to help take care of him half the time since he wasn't really able to walk. Yaseer dug his phone out and was about to call Paris to come home early from her trip at the mall with her sister but quickly vetoed the idea. It was going to be hard enough for her to come home and see them there. Now she had no choice but to look at the proof of his infidelities every time she walked through the door. He figured he could delay that for at least another hour or so. He decided it would be best to use his other option, his brothers. Yaseer called Zyon and Liam on three-way.

Once they were both on the line, he only said one line, "I need you at my house now," before disconnecting the call. No other words were needed. He knew that they knew from his tone that he really needed them.

Ten minutes later, his brothers were walking through his door one behind the other. As soon as they walked through the door, they stopped dead in their tracks, both with shocked expressions on their faces.

"Aw shit," Liam muttered out. He already knew some shit was about to go down when Paris got home. Yeah she loved kids but being around Yaseer's side pussy's children would be a totally different battle.

"I know, bruh, but ain't nun I can do. Somebody dropped them and they stuff off at my door and I ain't turning my back on my seeds for nobody, not even for...Paris," Yaseer called out in a low tone as he saw her standing in the doorway.

"What's going on? Why y'all got the door open? And you not turning your back on who, even for me? Come on, Yaseer. Don't get silent now. You was just doing a lot of yakking a few seconds ago. Come on, Daddy. Tell me what the biz is."

"Move out the way Zy and Lee so she can see who will always come before her and who I will never turn my back on, not even for her," Yaseer spat.

Zyon and Liam parted like the Red Sea so that Paris could so who Yaseer was talking about. Paris looked down and saw the precious faces she had seen that day in the restaurant, when her world had come crumbling down. That was the day that she found out about Yaseer's infidelities and secret family, so to say. But being the woman she was, she could never take out any of her hurt feelings against those beautiful angles because it was not their fault. The blame fell on Yaseer for stepping out on her while she did his bid, and for him to think that she would even go against him for being a part of his children's lives showed how much he really knew her. Paris bit the inside of her bottom lip to try and keep herself from crying. How could Yaseer even think so low of her?

"Damn bae, you really think that low of me? You really think I would even ask you to put me before your seeds? I would think less of you as a man if you did because a real man takes care of his responsibilities first. And these little ones need all the love and care they can receive, especially with their mother being six feet under. I don't expect them to pay the price for your fuck ups because they are innocent. Don't you ever put my character into question again. You should know me better than that." With those last words passing through her lips, she walked off into the direction of their bedroom to put up her new items that she had picked up at the mall.

Yaseer sat there in shock that she had just handled him yet again. This was the second time she handled him like his name was Raggedy Ann. But he really couldn't be mad at her because he really had thought she would flip out. Paris could go from zero to one hundred and you wouldn't even see it coming. So yeah, in a way he did question her character, and for that he felt he owed her an apology.

He rolled down to the room they had been sleeping in while he had been in his chair, since he couldn't get up and down the stairs to their room. He had made a mental note to add an elevator in his mini mansion. He was at the door when he heard the shower water running. He turned back around and decided to wait until she came out to talk to her.

Chapter 8

Heartbreaker

Three hours later, Zyon and Liam were gone. Yaseer and Paris had talked their feelings out and Paris was in the room asleep, along with the girls. Yaseer picked up the girls' bags and a square shaped envelope fell out of the side. Yaseer frowned up his face as he bent down as far as he could and picked the envelope up. The envelope was addressed to him. In the inside of it was an unmarked DVD.

Yaseer rolled down the hall to his office and got his portable DVD player so that he could see what was on the DVD out of curiosity. He slid the disc inside of it. A blue screen popped up with the words "The Naked Truth" highlighted in yellow and the time length of the video beside it. Yaseer pressed play. A blacked out figure came on the screen sitting in a chair. Yaseer scrunched his brows up in confusion as to who the hell this was and what they wanted with him, better yet how they knew him and where to reach him. As soon as the first line left his mouth, Yaseer knew exactly who it was.

Yaseer's eyes were glued to the screen in disbelief. In less than ten minutes, Yaseer's blood went from warm to past

47

boiling as he sat and listened to this nigga go on to explain a secret about Paris that had his heart breaking and him an emotional wreck. Yaseer hated to be deceived and lied to. He felt as though he had been betrayed. The code he always preached to his crew, as well as her, was Loyalty, Honesty, and Respect. She had just broken all three.

"Fuck her," Yaseer screamed as he used the back of his hand and arm to swipe everything off of his desk. For the first time in a long time, Yaseer cried like a baby. To him, this was a fate worse than death because he loved Paris more than he loved himself. She was the last person he expected to do him dirty. Yaseer gathered his composure. He had something for her ass. She wanted to do him dirty like this, well two could play that game.

Yaseer called the crew and set up a group meeting at The Chambers. They would convene in two weeks. It was going to be hard as hell for him to act like everything was all Gucci when it wasn't, but he had done it with Ezra when they were trapping him and could do it again. He was about to show her how his wrath felt. He had the perfect plan. If everything worked like he planned, it would turn out just right. Then, after he handled her, he was going to make it his mission to find out who made this tape and thought it smart to make sure he received this bullshit, and he was going to take their soul. Whoever it was had access to his daughters and that made him even madder.

What was even worse was that after Ariel got killed, none of his crew, including his brothers, even thought to seek out his daughters to make sure that they were okay. For over three months, they were in someone's house with God knows who around them.

Yaseer's blood was scolding hot. It was hotter than fish grease.

Two Weeks Later…

Paris was fiddling around, getting dressed and primped to go this meeting with Yaseer. She assumed it was the normal meetings they usually had to check their cash flow and bricks, and to make sure no one was trying to ease in on their territory. That was a big no-no. TTC ran Charlotte, NC and to get in their way was asking for a one way ticket to hell.

Paris secured her weapons and got ready to go. Yaseer had caught a ride with his brothers so that he could arrive a little early. Paris was ready to get the meeting over. Her pregnancy was kicking her behind and had her beyond tired, not to mention her helping take care of Madison and Chaunte. Brooklyn had planned to get them this weekend so she would get plenty of rest while they were gone. Surprisingly, things were going well with her and Yaseer since the babies had moved in. Or so she thought.

"Mrs. Adela, I'm about to leave. There are fresh bottles in the refrigerator for the girls. Their night clothes are on my bed. And if they get fussy, just give them their binkies and hum them a tune. Oh, and make sure you put their diaper cream on their bottoms so they don't get a rash. And please, please make sure there is nothing in their cribs that can suffocate them. Make sure you place them on their sides so if they puke because of their acid reflux, they won't asphyxiate on their own vomit." Paris shot out demands as she descended down the stairs.

"I know all of this. I have six kids and three grandbabies. If it's anything I know how to do, it is take care of babies. Now hurry up fo you be late to your date with that handsome young man of yours. You know he hates when you're late," she spoke with a southern drawl in her words.

"I know, I know" Paris said as she bent down and gave the girls a kiss on their chubby cheeks. She had grown quite fond of them. If someone had told her a year ago that she would be raising children Yaseer had outside of their relationship, she would have sent them to meet their maker immediately, without any hesitation or regard. But here she was caring for them as if they were her own flesh and blood.

She looked over her shoulder, flashed a smile, and then walked out the door and got into her blacked out Chrysler 200 to go meet up with the crew.

Twenty minutes later, she was pulling up at the spot where they brought people to make their exit out of the world. Paris got of her car and adjusted her black cameo top. A warm breeze blew by causing her hair to blow into her face and making some strands get caught in the stickiness of her lip gloss. She pulled them back and made her way inside of the warehouse looking building, stopping her stride once more to adjust the waistband of her maternity jeans before continuing inside.

Paris walked down the middle hall of The Chambers, passing the room doors that had special ways inside them that sent their enemy's to hell in a handbasket. At the end of the hall were big black double doors that led to the conference room. Paris walked into the room seeing that she was the last one to arrive. She said her hello's to everyone as she sat down in the chair that was on the right side of the chair Yaseer usually sat in. He had not come in yet and it seemed as though everyone was waiting on him.

After five minutes of everyone chatting and catching up with one another, the door opened and in came Yaseer in his wheel chair with Zyon behind him. As soon as the door was closed, Yaseer turned his wheelchair to face his crew. He adjusted his silk black tie, and then locked the wheels of his chair.

"How's everyone doing?" Yaseer greeted.

Cool, straight, Gucci, and a'ight were some of the various responses that he received back.

"That's good to know. Bae, could you please pull my chair at the table back for me a little bit."

"Sure thing, hun," Paris replied as she obliged his request.

"Thanks love," Yaseer responded. "Let's get this meeting underway, shall we. Tonight will not be our typical meeting. Tonight, this meeting is dedicated to someone very special to me, my heartbeat, the woman who is carrying my seeds, my love, my other half, my rib, Paris."

Paris looked at Yaseer a little discombobulated before her full lips spread into a beautiful smile, revealing a pretty set of straight white teeth.

"Yas—" She was stopped in the midst of calling Yaseer's name when he held up his hand to silence her.

"Let me finish, bae. This meeting tonight is all about you, love. Just sit back, be pretty, and save yo breath for my seeds," he said with smirk as he ran his massive hands over his fresh Caesar cut.

For the first moment since Yaseer had come into the room, Paris noticed he had cut his hair that had grown out to shoulder length in beautiful curls, his chin hair was shaped up and all. Her man was not only a boss but looked the part.

"Zy, can you hand me the remote to the TV and DVD player?" Yaseer asked his brother Zyon.

Zyon walked over to where the sixty-inch plasma TV was mounted on the wall and grabbed the remotes out of the black and gold wooden cabinets under the TV. Then he walked over to Yaseer and handed them to him.

"Aye Zy, can you hand me that black knapsack hanging on the hook behind you?"

Zyon looked at Yaseer trying to figure out if he had lost his mind with all of the request, but obliged him none the less. Yaseer reached in the knapsack and pulled out some gummy worms, opened the bag, and bit off one the worm shaped gummies. He closed his eyes and savored the sweetness of it before looking over at his crew.

"Oh, my bad, I'm holding shit up, huh? Let me turn the lights down for the movie."

Yaseer picked the TV remote up off his lap, pointed the TV remote at the TV, and turned it on. After doing so, he reached back in the knapsack and took out a tiny remote. He raised the hand that held the remote up to the ceiling and pressed a button on it. The room darkened slowly as it would do in an actual movie theatre. Once the menu screen to the movie popped up, Yaseer pressed play, sat back in his wheelchair and put another gummy worm between his teeth.

Chapter 9

Exposure

"Sup Yaseer, you know I couldn't just leave in peace, didn't ya? Well, well, well, if ya watching this then that means my black ass must be dead. Damn, I can't believe I slipped up. I should have killed your ass years ago when yo peeps got popped by the feds. Speaking of your peeps, well technically my peeps too, it's fucked up how they got handed that whack ass life sentence, huh? I couldn't believe that shit. Oh, wait, yes I could because I had a hand in it. I gathered up all the information I could, gift wrapped that shit, and sent it to the feds. The funny thing is he might have gotten off if the judge had not of found out our pops was banging his wife. I wonder who told him that. Oh my bad, again it was me. This damn memory of mine just be slipping in and out. Your pops would have probably gotten off light since they had the judge in their pockets but... well you know what happened. Now see my problem is yeah I got my beefs with you and yeah I did some shady shit, but I wasn't fucking you either. I'm just curious as to how the woman who claims to love you, that she's down for you, sucking you off and fucking you every night, can sit up there in your face every fuckin' day knowing

damn well that her pussy ass father was the one who put your peeps on lock for life all because his dick couldn't satisfy his fuckin' wife and ain't say jack diddly squat to you about the moment she found out about who her piece of shit sperm donor was. I know I did my shit, hell I even had ya folks thinking it was they manz that set 'em up. Nope, it was me. I really didn't expect for them to give ma dukes that much time though, but oh well, it is what it is. And one more thing, watch ya back partna, I know you ain't think I was going out quietly and going to leave y'all in peace. Watch ya back homie because somebody will most definitely be watching you," Ezra said as the screen went black.

Yaseer used the tiny remote to turn the lights back on. All eyes were on Paris like Janet Jackson at the Super Bowl when her chichi popped out. The sound of someone clapping pulled them somewhat out of there haze. They looked at Yaseer like he was on something sitting there clapping, showing all thirty-two teeth.

"Now that right there, my nigga, that right there was some good shit," Yaseer said as he finished off the last gummy worm in the bag. He held the bag up and looked at it.

"Damn, I'm out of gummy worms? No, no, no this won't do. I got to get another bag ASAP, can't live without them," he said as he leaned over and threw the empty rapper in the trash that was in a corner beside him. "Did y'all enjoy the movie? Interesting shit, huh?" Yaseer asked as he checked to make sure the wheels on his chair were locked before grasping on to the arms of the wheelchair and standing up.

He was a little unsteady at first, before he got his footing. He worked extra hard in therapy to make this possible and now he was almost back to his full potential. The room was quiet as they looked on in shock. They didn't know rather to go in on Paris or celebrate Yaseer being able to stand on his feet again. Yaseer brushed a hand over his pin striped suit before placing his hands in his pants pockets.

"Alright now, not everyone speak at once. I mean that was some A1 shit right there. Yo ma, you did yo thang. I should make some calls to my connects and have a Grammy sent to yo ass for best deceiving, conniving, dishonest, wouldn't know respect if it hit her in the ass, disloyal bitch because you did that shit, girl. You did that, ma. I should've brought some wine to toast in your honor," Yaseer spat with a hint of amusement in his voice as he walked to the table and braced his hands on it as he looked his crew over before his eyes settled on Paris.

"Yaseer, wa—wait le—let me explain before you jump to any conclusions. It's not wh—"

"Don't you dare let 'It ain't what you think' slip out

57

ya mouth or I swear I'ma forget you pregnant with my seeds and knock yo ass out. Matter fact don't say shit else. Yo ass couldn't say shit when it was something I should have known three years ago when we got serious about one another so don't say shit now!"

"But Yas— it's—"

"Shu up. Shut da fuck up. How long did you plan on keeping this from me? Why the fuck did I have to find some shit out from a dead man, something yo breathing, lying ass should have told me from day one? Huh? Say something dammit," Yaseer yelled as tears began to well up in his eyes, but he refused to let them drop.

"Yaseer if you would give me a chance to exp-"

"You know what? I don't even want to hear it right now. Just take yo shit that I got packed outside the door and get the fuck out of my presence."

"You're not putting me out of my damn house, Yaseer. You can be mad all you want. You better take yo ass in the next room until you come to your senses and listen to my side of the story."

"Your house? I own that. I'm the one who paid for that, not you."

"And yo muthafuckin' ass wouldn't have been able to pay for shit if it had not been for me taking your bid. I did

58

that shit out of love. I did that to show you that I would risk it all, go to the ends of the earth fo yo ass. If I was that close to my fuckin' sperm donor, then my black ass wouldn't have seen a day in jail, let alone dating you. Did you forget where you met me? I was staying with my damn aunt, not my mother or my father, my fuckin aunt, Yaseer. In any of those times, did you ever see my father come visit me? Didn't you see me go hungry many a day because my aunt didn't always have money to buy food? My father's a fuckin' judge but I was rocking clothes from Crisis Ministry that people donated because they didn't want them anymore. So excuse the hell out of me for not keeping up with my dad's dirty life in the judicial system. I just found out about five months ago that my father was the one who tried your parent's case when I happened to be trying to locate him to make amends. And while you're throwing out words like disloyal, dishonest, deceiving, conniving, and respect, make sure you say the same shit to yourself because if it hadn't been for your cheating and getting the broad pregnant while I was doing time for your gun charge, then my ass wouldn't have left to stay in a hotel and would have never gotten raped. The only reason why I didn't tell you was because I found out the day that the shooting went down at A1. I had planned to tell you when we went home that night but shit happened to prevent that. Then after that, shit was like a never-ending battle so excuse the fuck out of me for trying to keep your head clear so you could find out who was trying to kill us. Matter of fact, fuck you and this shit. I'm gone. You ain't even got to worry about me or my unborn children. We will be just fine without yo' ass," Paris screamed with tears running down her face as she stood up and prepared to leave. She made it three steps before everything started spinning, went black, and she passed out.

Chapter 10

Open

"Paris," London screamed as she practically jumped out of her chair and ran to her sister's aid. London kneeled down on her hands and knees and lifted Paris' head into her lap.

"Somebody help, don't just look dammit," she yelled, looking at everybody before her eyes landed on Yaseer and her temper spiked through the roof.

"The fuck yo bama ass standing there looking in shock fo? This shit is yo fuckin' fault. Yo mouth was running a mile a minute two seconds ago. Don't get silent now. Fuck, my sister could be dying and y'all standing here looking like boo-boo the fool," London spat as she pulled her cell phone out to call the ambulance.

It was like that was all it took to get everybody in action. Liam and Zyon came running over to Paris' aid. Zyon picked her up, Liam grabbed her belongings, and they fled the building to the car to get an unresponsive Paris to the hospital.

Yaseer stood there in shock trying to figure out what had just happened and how things went so bad so fast. Yes, he had planned to embarrass her as well as kick her out of the house, but he did not expect for her to pass out. He went from being mad to scared that she was going to die. Any time it came to Paris leaving his house, something happened. Maybe this was a sign from God or something.

"Yo, Seer, Seer," Kai'yan called out. "Come on, we got to get to the hospital, man, to make sure P and the babies okay" Kai'yan said.

Yaseer stood up to his full height and walked as fast as his body would allow out of the chambers. His body wasn't strong enough to run but he was trying his best.

Two hours later...

Yaseer's head popped up when he saw a tall African American doctor come strolling toward the section that the crew was seated in.

"Are anyone of you a Yaseer Davis?" the doctor inquired as he eyed the teary-eyed bunch.

"Yes, I am Yaseer," Yaseer said as he rose up slowly from his seat and shook the doctor's extended hand.

"Hi, I'm Doctor Yakubu, Paris' OB-GYN. Okay, so the good news is that mom and babies are going to be fine. However, Paris' blood pressure was very high and that is what caused her to pass out. She has a condition called preeclampsia, which is high blood pressure while she is pregnant. The thing that is most important in her case, as well as the babies, is for her to stay stress free in order to keep her and the babies out of danger. She needs to modify her diet to a low sodium diet. I will discuss these things with her when she wakes up as well. I'm going to keep her overnight just for observation, to make sure her blood pressure is stable before I send her home."

"Thanks, Doc," Yaseer responded as he nodded his head up and down, taking everything in at one time.

It was going to be difficult to keep the way he felt about finding out who Paris' father was in check. Every time he saw her, he would think about her not being upfront with him. He was trying his hardest to see her reasons for not telling him but it did nothing to heal the re-opened wounds. He also knew that he was going to have to find a way to keep his feelings in check because the last thing he needed was something happening to his babies or Paris. No matter how mad he was at her, that didn't change the love he had in his heart for her.

Maybe it would be best for her to stay at London's, Yaseer thought to himself. Yeah, yeah, that's a good idea, he thought but then vetoed his own idea. Naah, I need to be able to keep an eye on her 24/7. London might let her get away with eating things she shouldn't eat. Then she would be worried 'bout me. Yaseer argued back and forth with himself in his head. He finally came up with the solution. He would let Paris live in the house and make sure it was only stocked with healthy foods. Then he would rent out a place for him to stay in. He felt like that was being more than fair, as well as looking out for Paris and keeping her healthy at the same time.

"Thank y'all for coming up here. Y'all can go ahead and leave. I'ma stay here with P tonight to keep an eye on her. Aye, Zy, when they release her tomorrow, you think you can roll through and scoop us up?"

"Yeah bruh, you ain't even have to ask," Zyon replied in his baritone voice.

"A'ight, that's what's up. I'ma get at y'all later, let me go on back here with my shawty," Yaseer said. Then he remembered he shouldn't be calling her his anymore. That is going to take a lot of getting used to, he thought to himself as turned and headed for Paris' room.

Yaseer inhaled a deep breath before he pushed Paris' room door open and went in. His breath caught seeing her plugged up to an IV and her hooked up to the baby monitor. He didn't like seeing her like that. He grabbed the chair that was stationed by the closet in her room, pulled it close to her bed, and sat down beside her. At first, he just sat there staring at her beautiful face before he let his emotions spill out of his mouth.

"Yo P, I swear I ain't mean for no shit like this to happen. I knew what I was doing when I sat this up, but I had no clue it would turn out like this. I thought exposing and kicking you out would make me feel better, but it didn't. If anything, it made me feel even worse than before. I heard what you said back there and I can even reason with you waiting to tell me. But bae, you got to understand this is a tough pill for me to swallow. I mean I often wonder if my parents had not got sentenced by your father, would I have had to lead the lifestyle I lead. I could have been a doctor, or went off to the air force or something like that. The point is I would be living stress free. You would have never had to do my time, and I would have never gotten stabbed because I would have never met Ariel, But then again, I wouldn't have met you either. I don't know P. I'm so confused. I don't know how to feel or what to do. This shit eating me up, ma," Yaseer said as he placed his elbows on his knees and his head in between his massive hands covering his face.

Tears fell down Yaseer's face as he thought about how much Ezra had ruined his life. Yes, her dad was supposed to let them off light being that he worked for his parents. But at the same time, the majority of the blame landed on a man that was already dead. He wished he could breathe life back into him and then take his life again. One question plagued his mind. Who had his daughters? If he could find that out, then he could find out who put the tape in their bag, how they knew Ezra, and how the hell they knew how to find him.

Chapter 11

Who?

Yaseer sat up with fresh thoughts in his head. First thing in the morning, he was linking up with the team to get the search for this mystery person underway. He could practically smell the blood of his next victim. His head was filled with thoughts on how he would torture his next victim to death. Maybe dismembering them piece by piece with a chainsaw while they were still breathing, the thought of peeling Their skin off limb by limb crossed his mind, or maybe putting them in their specially made shower and dowsing his victim in acid. He was getting excited just thinking about it. An idea popped in his head. He finally came up with the perfect way to torture and kill his next victim. Yaseer rubbed his hands in anticipation as a sinister smile crept upon his lips.

"Aww hell, yo crazy ass got that look?" Paris said in a sleep filled voice.

Yaseer's head snapped over to see his heart with her eyes open staring at him through lowered lids.

Damn, I can't stay mad at her for shit, he thought to himself, all the while thanking the heavens that she was okay. Fuck that, we not living apart. Hell nah, Yaseer pondered to himself as he continued to gaze at Paris.

"What, Yaseer? Stop looking at me like that, shit scary as hell," Paris spat, looking at Yaseer sideways.

A smile spread across his full lips causing all thirty-two to show. He was happy that she was still alive and healthy. He was determined they would work through their problems, wasn't no leaving shit happening. After today he realized how short life is and he honestly couldn't fathom his life without her in it. Yaseer didn't say a word. He just leaned in close to her face, stared at her plush lips for a split second, and then leaned in some more and kissed her soft lips, adding a little tongue before he pulled back a little bit.

"Don't you ever scare me like that again, ma," Yaseer said to Paris as he looked her in her eyes.

"It wasn't intentional. You had not only pissed me off, but hurt and humiliated me, so I just wanted to get the hell up out of that building as fast as I could. Then next thing I know, I wake up in this room." Yaseer did not feel like reliving those events in his head so he changed subjects.

"I spoke with your OB doc. He said you have a condition called preeclampsia. Ma, ion need shit happening to you and my seeds. That stress shit got to go, and I'm going to try my hardest not to stress you out. My feelings ain't shit compared to the breath of you and my unborns. Oh yeah, them hot pork skins, pickles, Doritos, hot pockets and shit got to go, too. That shit raise your blood pressure as well. So salads, baked meat, and fruit for you, my dear," Yaseer said as he rubbed Paris' growing abdomen.

"Damn, I hate he told you that," Paris groaned out.

Well, there went her cravings down the drain. She already knew Yaseer was about to be twelve when it came to the food she ate from here on out. Anything she ate with salt before would now be deemed a crime in Yaseer's head. Yaseer's hand ceased movement as he looked dead at her with a serious expression on his face

"You knew about your condition and didn't tell me?" he spat as he removed his hand from her abdomen.

"Yyyaaass, 'cause yo ass be taking shit to the extreme sometimes, just like you did when you watched that video and then decided to embarrass me instead of coming to me about it like a real man should have done. And you wonder why I didn't tell you about the preeclampsia. Would that have stopped you from your temper exploding when you saw the video and causing you to throw one big ass temper tantrum, or nah? And since we exposing all my shit today, here's another one that will put the icing on the cake for ya. These babies may or may not be yours."

Yaseer stood up ready to explode, but Paris silenced

him with her hand.

"Hold on, papi. Before you go C4 on my ass, I need you to listen to me."

"Bit-"

"Before you say that word, think about it. I could call you bitches all day for having two kids outside of our relationship with a dolla dick suckin' hoe. According to dates, I got pregnant around the time Ezra did what he did to me. You do remember that don't you? Yeah, I know you do. Anyways, you and I had just had sex the day that he raped me so now can you see where the confusion comes in as to who's the pappy?" Paris spat with her eyebrows raised up and a sarcastic smile on her face.

Yaseer felt like someone had punched him in his stomach and stole his breath. He hadn't forgotten about the rape, and he never would. But he was so happy that she was expecting that he didn't even sit back and think that the unborn children may not even be his. Suddenly, what he had been mad at her for earlier seemed like a mustard seed compared to this. How the hell was he going to deal if the babies he had grown to love before they were even born weren't even his, much less his ex-best friend's, his brother/cousin, his dead enemy Ezra.

Yaseer got sick to his stomach. He could feel the contents that he had consumed earlier that day reversing their way up his digestive system. Yaseer jumped up, ran to the bathroom, and puked up the contents in his stomach. Yaseer balanced his elbows on the brim of the toilet bowl. He took a few deep breaths to try and get himself together. He stood up, went to the sink, and washed his mouth out. Then he dried his mouth off with a paper towel. He stood there looking himself in the mirror, willing himself to get it together. Yaseer brushed a hand over his waves and walked out of the bathroom back to where Paris was.

"Hey um I'ma dip out for a little minute. I'll be back later. Love ya," he said as he bent down, kissed Paris on the forehead, and then left out. Fuck waiting til tomorrow, he was going to get answers about who put that DVD in the twins' baby bag starting now. That DVD practically ripped the hat off of Pandora's Box, Yaseer thought to himself.

Chapter 12

Gone

"Aye Zy, come scoop me up from the hospital. We got some stuff we need to figure out," Yaseer said and then disconnected the call. He sent a mass message to the crew telling them to meet him at his house. He needed something to ease his mind right about now and had the perfect thing for it as soon as he got home. Ten minutes later, Zyon pulled up in his all-black Yukon sitting on twenty-twos.

"Whud up, bruh?" Zyon asked as he lightly put his foot on the gas and pulled off slowly, giving Yaseer time to put his seatbelt on. Once Yaseer was strapped in, he turned up Future's new song "Monster" and let the lyrics fill the space of the truck.

"Shiid a lot, bruh, too damn much if ya ask me. I'ma tell ya everything once we get to my house, but the main thing that's weighing on my mind now is who the fuck put that DVD in the twins' bag. Like that shit opened up a can of worms that I don't think I was ready for," Yaseer said as he leaned his head back on the headrest and closed his eyes.

The day had turned out worse than he thought it would. He hadn't been expecting to get back into the swing of things so quickly, but now things were moving full steam ahead.

"Who the hell else was in cahoots with Ezra? Whoever it is must know by now that he is dead and he had to give them some just-in-case instructions in order for them to know who you were and where you lived. Matter of fact, who the fuck had my nieces?" Zyon questioned as he pulled up to Yaseer's house.

They began getting out of the car and walking up the driveway. Yaseer was about to say something as he made movement to get out of the car, and then abruptly stopped his movement and closed the door back.

"Hol' up, fam. Sum ain't right. You know I always keep my porch light and foyer light on. Now look, my house pitch dark," Yaseer said as he pulled his .22 from his gun holster, took the lock off, and put one in the chamber. Zyon did the same with his .45. Yaseer looked over at his younger twin and nodded his head over to the side toward the window, signaling for Zyon to come on.

The two got out of the car and moved with the experience of a professional thief in the night, making sure to move quickly and as silently as possible. Yaseer got to the door a few seconds before Zyon and leaned his back against the brick wall of his home next to his front door with the business end of his gun facing the ground. His door was slightly ajar. Yaseer looked at Zyon silently communicating his love for his brother just in case something happened to either one of them when they went inside the house.

Yaseer eased toward the door. He used his foot to slowly push the door open, attempting to be as quiet as possible. Zyon was right behind him. They walked into the house, making sure to check their surroundings as they searched to see what was missing and if anyone was there.

"It's about time y'all got here. I been waiting on y'all forever. Please come get this fool out of my sight. I got two babies to look after," Adela said from the couch in the living room as she spotted Yaseer and

Zyon looking around for the intruder.

Yaseer flicked on the light switch, looked at Adela, and then at the guy who was on the floor with his hands and feet bound and duct tape across his mouth to keep him silenced.

"Adela, what the hell happened? Damn, my pops was definitely right about you. You ain't no joke."

"Ya damn skippy. I don't play when it comes to the little ones, as well as myself."

"I see. Now answer some questions for me. Did this idiot tell you why he was here or who sent him?"

74

"Naw, I figured you would be better at getting an answer out of him than I would."

"Where were you when he came in and are the girls okay?"

"I was actually coming out of the girls' room and about to come around the corner when I heard someone messing with the door knob. Then next thing I knew, a masked figure was walking through the door. Lucky for me, I was right near my room. So I eased in there, grabbed my nine, and eased back out. I saw him coming my way in the direction of the twins' room. I put my back against the wall and waited for the fool to come around the corner. When he did, I knocked him across the head with the butt of my gun, used some duct tape that I had to tape him all up, drug him to the living room, and voila. I sat and waited for y'all. His mistake was cutting off the lights when he came in. Had he not, he probably would have saw all two hundred twenty-five pounds of me," Mrs. Adela spat, laughing to herself as she recalled the events.

She had killed men for much less back when she worked with Yaseer's parents before they got arrested. Now her duty was to protect the Davis' grandchildren and son. When Yaseer's mom called with the request, she didn't hesitate to say yes.

"That's what's up. Thank you for protecting my girls. I will make sure to add a little something special to your check on Friday," he stated while he was locking and securing his gun in its rightful place.

"'Preciate it, but the extra not even needed. I enjoyed taking it to this young buck. He ain't even know what was coming. Now if you fellas will excuse me, I have some little ones to be looking after," Adela said as she got up preparing to go warm up the twins' bottle.

Boom. They heard the loud thud of something being knocked over in the direction of where the twins' room was.

"Adela, stay here and watch him," Yaseer yelled over his shoulder as he took off running to the girls' room to make sure they were alright.

Yaseer opened the door to the twins' room and stopped dead in his tracks. There window was open with a slight breeze blowing the curtains and both of the twins' beds were empty.

"Noooooo," Yaseer screamed as he ran to their beds as if they would magically reappear. When he got to Madison's bed, he noticed a folded sheet of paper lying inside of her crib. He picked it up, unfolded the sheet of paper, and read the words out loud but barely above a whisper.

"How does it feel to be tortured?" was all that it read

in permanent marker. Yaseer dropped the sheet of paper and fell to his knees. He felt like someone had snatched his soul from his body.

"Come on, bruh, we ain't going to be able to get the girls back if we stay here moping around. Let's go get the bastards who even brave enough to cross ya path, son," Zyon said as he helped Yaseer to his feet.

The two of them walked out of the twins' room ready to kill any and every one on sight. One wrong move could cost you your life.

Chapter 13
WTH

Yaseer and Zyon were almost to the door when Yaseer back peddled to the living room. He had almost forgotten about the man that was tied up in his living room being watched by Adela.

"Help me grab this fool, Zy. Either he gon give up some answers or he gone meet his maker," Yaseer said as he grabbed his next victim by his feet and started pulling him toward the door.

"Mrs. Adela, you may go home. The twins are not here so we no longer need your services. You are relieved," Yaseer said as he continued dragging the guy to the door, not paying attention to her rebuttal.

"Umm ummm," The man shouted as he started to come to. He blinked his eyes slowly as he realized that he was tied up and being dragged. He noticed Yaseer and started wriggling about.

He shook his head side to side as he tried to speak through the duct tape. Yaseer stopped pulling him for a brief second. He went to the guy's head and used the foot of his boot to knock him back unconscious, and then went back to pulling him. Zyon walked up and picked the guy up under his shoulders to help Yaseer carry him down the three porch steps and to the trunk of Zyon's truck. They were ready to put in work.

Yaseer took out his phone and called Kai'yan to tell him that they had a situation and to meet them down at the chambers. He dialed up Liam to tell him the same thing but Liam's phone kept going straight to voicemail.

"It would be like Liam to be balls deep in pussy at the wrong damn time. That's the only time that nigga don't charge his phone, when he with a bitch," Yaseer spat under his breath.

Once they got to the chambers, he would try to reach Liam one more time. If he couldn't reach him then, then fuck it. He didn't have time to be blowing up no niggas phone, not even his brother's. He had more important shit to handle, like finding his daughters.

Twenty minutes later, they were pulling up to the chambers ready to do damage. Kai'yan pulled up as they were climbing out of the car.

"Come on, bruh, let's get this nigga in here so we can get the info we need and go catch the nigga behind all this shit," Zyon said as he took off his TTC chain, as well as his crisp black tee, leaving him clad in a form fitting black wife beater, some dark blue True Religion jeans, and a fresh pair of black and red J's. The two brothers, along with Kai'yan, walked up to Zyon's trunk and popped it.

"So bruh, you wanna fill me in on what's going on?" Kai'yan asked.

"I will in a few. As of right now, let's get him inside and wake him up," Yaseer spat as he bent over and began to try and lift their mystery victim up.

"Say bruh, watch out. Let me and Kai'yan carry him. You know your back not all the way heeled yet," Zyon stated as he moved in to pick the mystery man up with Kai'yan on his heels helping him lift their unmasked victim.

They walked to the entrance of The Chambers and stood off to the side of the door so Yaseer could punch in the code. Once inside, they took him to the first room in the building, which was known as the waiting room. They sat him in the chair, cut the tape on his wrist and ankles, and then chained him to the chair. Once they had him secure, they took the tape off of the mouth part of the ski mask and pulled the mask off of the mystery man's head. All movement ceased for what seemed like forever.

"What the hell?" Yaseer muttered under his breath.

"Liam," Zyon spat softly.

They all looked on in surprise. They were as confused

as two left shoes. Yaseer walked out of the room for a split second and came back with a bucket of ice water. He held it up and poured it over his brother's head. Yaseer was determined to find out what the fuck was going on because this shit didn't make a lick of sense.

"Liam's head shot up from his bent position as he gasped for the air that the freezing water had taken away.

"The fuck, now yo' ass want people to wake up. When I was awake tryna get your attention to tell you that it was me and that your nanny is a crooked bitch, then you wanted to kick mofos in the face and shit.

"Well how the hell was I supposed to know it was you?" Yaseer replied.

"I said uuumm uuummm trying to get your attention."

"How the hell I'm supposed to understand uuummm uuummm? And hold up, what you mean my nanny crooked?"

"I'on know how you was supposed to understand me but I was hoping yo crazy as would, and just like I said nigga, your nanny is crooked as shit. I go over your house to check on my nieces since I knew you was at the hospital with Paris. So here I am doing my uncle duty about to check up on my nieces when I pulled up and noticed an unfamiliar car parked in the driveway. First off, if ya nanny fucking, that's nasty as shit, sitting there looking like a rejection of biggies sperm.

Second, no one that you don't know personally is allowed in your house, which I'm pretty sure you laid that out to her in the job description. Third, your foyer light wasn't even on and you keep that shit on religiously. Any who, something just didn't feel right so I pulled my gun, took the lock off of it, and put one in the chamber. I took my key out on the way to the door and went in the house, business end of my tool facing downwards but ready to bark at any time. I open the door and walked in. I intentionally kept the light off, hoping to catch whoever was doing what in the dark. I went down to the twins' room to check on them. I opened the door, walked in, looked in their cribs, and the twins was gone. I went to turn around to go find Adela to see what the fuck was going on. Then as soon as I turned, I was hit on the head with what seemed to look like a butt of a gun. It was her face that I saw before I blacked out. Next thing I saw when I woke up was you pulling me by my damn legs."

Yaseer's face contorted in one of the most hateful killer looks. He was on ten and ready to shoot. Fuck torturing, he wanted somebody's life now and not a second later.

"The fuck! And why the fuck you was wearing a mask dressed in all black."

"Nigga you know all black is our color so get the fuck out of here with all that rah rah. And I don't know how the shit got on my head. Didn't I just tell yo ass Precious laid my ass out with the butt of her gun?" Liam spat.

"Unchain him and let's go. We got a killah whale to catch," Yaseer said walking to the door. Then he stopped and turned around for a split second.

"Aye Kai'yan, can you go in my office and get me one of my black wife beaters, a black tee, my black sweats, and my black Timbs."

"Yeah I got you, bruh," Kai'yan replied knowing Yaseer probably wasn't ready to go into his office just yet and face the painful memories. Kai'yan left the room.

Five minutes later, he came back with Yaseer's requested items in his hands. Yaseer took them from him excused himself, went into the restroom across the hallway and changed out of his suit into his TTC gear.

Chapter 14

Killah

"A'ight, now I'm Gucci. Let's go get this old hoe," Yaseer said as he secured his gun in his gun holster.

"Let's ride," Liam said ready to get his revenge on. He was ready to push shawdy's wig back with the same gun that she hit him with.

The crew walked out to Kai'yan's blacked-out Hummer, ready for war. Yaseer didn't know why they were choosing to fuck with him but he had that work for them if they wanted it. He played no games. God help whoever was behind this and Lord have mercy on Adela, her as was his. She had been in his home for the past few weeks acting like she was the perfect nanny. Yaseer frowned as a thought popped into his head.

"Say bruh, why you making that face? What the hell done popped into that head of yours?" Kai'yan asked. He knew that face and that meant Yaseer had a question in his head that he was trying to figure out on his own.

"See the thing is my dad recommended Adela. She used to work for his organization. Why the fuck would he send me a crook? He had to know shawdy was shady. I mean, how could he not?"

"Did you detect she was shady after being in your home for almost three weeks?" Zyon questioned.

"Well no."

"So how you figure dad knew she was shady? I know for damn sure he wouldn't send no nut job into a house with his son, let alone his granddaughters. So get that crazy thought out cha brain, son," Zyon mugged a little after he finished his statement. One thing he knew was that his pops wasn't shady. A lady's man yes, but shady hell no and Yaseer should have known that just like he did.

The ride was silent as they rode back to Yaseer's house. Yaseer was praying that Adela was still there but he had a feeling that she wasn't. Good thing he had hidden cameras throughout his house. He never had much use for them before because no one was ever brave enough to fuck with him on the home front. But he was grateful that he had them because right now he needed all the clues he could get to find his daughters.

They pulled into Yaseer's circular driveway, parked, and hopped out ready for whatever.

As they got closer to the door, they noticed broken glass and yet again his door was slightly ajar. One by one the crew pulled there tools ready to blast off at any sudden movement. Yaseer used his foot to push the door open. He was hoping someone would jump out so he could blast their ass to kingdom come.

Broken glass cracked beneath their feet as they walked into the house. Yaseer flicked on the light in the foyer to bring light to the situation. He looked about his house, scanning over the mess that it had become. His house was beyond trashed, it was literally in shambles. It was like they were looking for something, but what? But then again, it looked like a mad person had just lost their mind for a quick second and tore shit up for the hell of it.

They walked throughout the house searching for Adela or whoever else might be in the house along with her. Once they saw that the house was clear, the crew headed to Yaseer's home office. They needed a hint as to what happened with the girls. Yaseer took out his keys to his office and opened the door up. They all gathered inside. Liam shut the door as he entered last.

Yaseer went to his dresser drawer, pulled out a remote, and pressed a small button. The wall behind him parted in two and there set multiple lit up TV screens with different angles of Yaseer's house, from different views of the outside to views of every room in the house. His cameras literally where aimed to catch every little thing. The high quality equipment captured the tiniest things. Yaseer walked over to the TVs and started fumbling with buttons, rewinding the tapes back so he could see everything from the time that Liam came in to the time Adela left.

Yaseer grabbed his black high backed rolling chair from his desk and sat down in it as he scanned over the cameras looking for the exact moment that the twins were kidnapped.

Yaseer looked on carefully for what seemed like minutes, but was actually seconds. Then boom, there it was. He watched Adela give the babies to someone outside of the window. As far as she knew, Yaseer only had a camera at the front door, which was visible to anyone. However she didn't know about the ones he had hidden.

Yaseer then watched as Liam came inside of the house without a mask and went in search of the twins as he had told him. He also witnessed Adela knocking Liam out, going in what seemed like a handbag, pulling a ski mask out, and placing it over Liam's head while he was unconscious. She then bound his wrists and ankles with duct tape and pulled him by his feet to the living room. It looked like she struggled a little to do it but she got it done.

The next thing Yaseer saw was himself walking into the house. He fast-forwarded to the part where they heard the loud thud in the twins' room. It looked as though someone had come back to drop the note in the crib. Attempting to hurry up and get back out in a flash, he tripped and fell over his own footing in a haste to get out, knocking something over in the process.

That was the loud thud that everyone heard. Last but not least, Yaseer caught the license plate of the vehicle the twins were in and the license plate of the car that Adela got into.

"A'ight, this how shit 'bout to go. Kai'yan, take these plate numbers and find out who these whips belong to. Zyon, track down Adela. She could be with whomever the car belongs to so you might as well tag along with Kai'yan. Liam, I need you to get some info on who put that DVD in the twins' bag and how they knew where I lived. Better yet, find out who had the twins in the first place while I was in my coma. I'm going to go check on Paris, as well as set up a meeting with the connect because our supply is getting low. I'm also gonna put my feet to the pavement to see who might know anything. On Tuesday, I plan to take a trip to Riker's to see Dad and find out about this woman he sent to my fuckin' house," Yaseer spat as he got up and grabbed the keys to his Chrysler 300. He needed to go be with Paris if only for an hour before he got out in these streets doing what he did best, wreak havoc.

The crew began disbursing with Yaseer first to hop in his whip, followed by Liam, Kai'yan, and then Zyon. Once on the highway, they all went their separate ways.

Liam was going to do what he was told but first he had a stop to make. He turned up Yo Gotti's old joint entitled "That's What's Up" and bobbed his head to the music as he got his head in killer mode. The first person that even looked like they were going to pop off stupid would be the person he would pop back with his tool. He may have been somewhat the pretty boy of the crew, but there was no bitch in him whatsoever. His blood was hot as fire but he wasn't even going to let his anger control him right now. He would have his revenge. He was going to make sure his face was the last one Adela saw when she inhaled her last breath.

Chapter 15

Fiyah

Liam pulled up in London's driveway and practically jumped out of the car before he even had the car in park and turned off. He was beyond mad at himself right now. He banged on London's door willing her to answer immediately. London opened the door with her .45 in her hand pointed at Liam's dome ready to blast off.

"Oh shit. Fool, don't be bangin' on my door like you the Jakes. I was ready to go out like Cleo on Set It Off," she said, referring to her favorite movie. She stepped back out of the way to let him in as she put her trigger happy hand down. She closed the door behind him. Then she walked past him to go do what she had been doing prior to him interrupting her, laying on her bed watching her Scandal series.

She flopped down on her bed belly first preparing to get back into one of her favorite television shows. That Olivia Pope is a bad bitch, she thought to herself as she got comfortable on her California King with a pillow under her forearms and her chin resting on them.

Liam stood in the doorway with his arms folded across his chest as eyeballed her seminude body. She was rocking some black leggings, a purple sports bra, and some black footies with her hair pinned up in a messy bun on the top of her head.

Liam uncrossed his arms and walked over to her massive bed. He was getting angrier and angrier at himself with every step he took. He had more important shit to do, like helping locate his nieces, but his body was disobeying his head at the present moment. He just needed a little relief before he went on a killing spree to get the answers he needed. Liam approached the bed and stood there for a split second before going into action. He leaned over, grabbed her by her upper arm, and flipped her over bringing his body on top of hers.

"The hel-" London started but was hushed by Liam's lips. His kiss was a little aggressive, as were his hands. He pulled her bottom lip in between his teeth as he continued to kiss her like it was their last kiss. His left hand gripped her right breast, then glided down the side of her body to her thick hips, and on down to her thighs. He grabbed her leg and placed it over his lean waist. He grinded his hips between her thighs.

That wasn't enough, he needed more. He needed to feel her. His fingers trailed up to the waistband of her leggings and he began sliding them down her legs. London lifted her hips a little so that he could get the leggings past her ass. Liam broke the kiss so he could get her leggings off of her. His breath almost caught in his throat ass he noticed she didn't have on any panties. His dick rocked up harder at the sight of her pretty pussy.

He stood up and kicked his black and red J's off, and then took his sweats and boxer briefs off. His black tee and TTC chain followed the rest of his clothes to the floor. He climbed back in between London's thighs with his member aiming at his goal. He pushed into her moist kitty, going all the way to the hilt. He eased back out only to push back in harder. He repeated the process over and over again.

London moved her hips up and down to match his thrust. She grabbed the back of his head and pulled his head down to her neck. Liam let his tongue out to taste her sweet flesh as he continued to pump.

"Shit," London moaned out. She gripped his head a little tighter. His roughness was turning her on even more and had her pussy leaking like a faucet.

"Harder, Liam, harder. Fuck me, fuck this pussy," London chanted.

Liam was on ten and ready to bust off. Her dirty talking had him pumping even harder and faster. He pulled out and flipped her over on her stomach.

"Toot that ass up, shawdy. You already know the deal," he spat.

London eagerly followed his instructions, more than ready for him to put that D on her. London bit her bottom lip and looked over her shoulder as Liam inserted his steel back inside of her tight wet walls. He began pumping slowly at first picking up momentum little by little. He gripped her hips as he pumped harder. He tilted his head back and swore to himself as he enjoyed the feel of London's womanhood. Sweat dripped down his abs as he began putting in overtime. He lifted his head back up and looked at his pipe go in and out of London's juicy pussy. The sight was a beaut. He smacked one of her caramel colored ass cheeks making it turn red in the process.

"Mmmm," London moaned out.

He grabbed ahold of her messy bun that had begun to fall out of place and pulled her head back as he pumped faster and faster. He felt his nut coming and he could tell it was going to be a massive one.

"I'm cummin', uh, uh oh shit," London hollered out, as she squirted all over Liam's stick.

Feeling her walls contract around his tool was all it took for his load to shoot off deep inside of her womb. He gripped her hips and held on as he emptied himself inside of her. The movements ceased as each tried to catch their breath. However, as much as Liam would like to sit and enjoy being deep inside of London and cuddling with her, they had work to do. He already knew she was going to curse him, as well as Kai'yan, Zyon, and Yaseer, for taking so long to tell her about the girls. That was his intent but his body out won the bottle of what he was supposed to be handling at the moment. He pulled out of her and got to his feet.

"Aye ma, come on. Let's go wash up so we can put some clothes on and get going. We got some major shit we need to handle."

London lifted her head up and looked at him over her shoulder thinking, How the fuck we got some major shit to handle and you wasting time dicking me down? But at the same time, as much as she wanted to be mad at him, she couldn't because it felt so good.

"What you mean major shit?"

Liam exhaled as he sat down on the edge of the bed so he could fill her in on what was going on from the incident that happened with him and Adela, on down to the twins, and finally to TTC taking him to the chambers and finding out it was him under the ski mask. Just as he thought she would, London exploded like a firecracker.

"Why the fuck are you just now telling me this? Matter of fact, why didn't anyone call me when the shit went down? See this the shit I'm talking about. Yaseer ass wanna call a meeting to try and embarrass Paris but can't pick up a phone to call and tell me about some real shit. That's that bullshit. Finding out that shit about my sister and her dad was something he could have dealt with in private, without involving people who didn't have shit to do with it. But when he need to call folks to tell them something major done happened, his ass can't do that. You know what? Fuck him and fuck you too. Move out my damn way so I can go take a shower and find out what the hell I need to do to help find them precious little babies," London said as she shoved Liam and jumped up out of the bed. She hadn't even gotten a step before Liam was on his feet, had grabbed her by her arm, and pushed her little ass into the nearest wall with his hand clasped around her neck.

"What the hell I told you about questioning my brother and his choices? If you got a problem with how shit is handled, then you can get yo' shit and go. Now as for your sister, no we didn't have no business being pulled into that shit, but we were. So let that shit go and cool the fuck out. My intent was to come over here and fill you in on what was going on and scoop you up, but for some reason," Liam paused and lightly pecked

London's pouting lips before finishing his statement. "I couldn't control my damn hormones. Now calm yo' lil' ass down. Come on, let's take a shower so we can get dressed and handle business," Liam spat as he let her go and stalked off to the bathroom so that he could go wash up, leaving London and her thoughts standing there in the nude.

Chapter 16

Info

London stepped out of the shower dripping wet, followed by Liam. She pulled a fluffy white towel off of the towel rack, opened it up, wrapped it around her chest, and tucked it so that it wouldn't fall off. Liam pulled a towel off of the same rack and tied it around his waist, tucking his as well to make sure it stayed in place.

London walked out of the bathroom into her bedroom and sat down at her vanity mirror. She took her black paddle brush and combed through her curly wet hair. She put a little bit of Gorilla Snot gel in her hand and put it around the perimeter of her hair to hold her unruly curls in tack. After that, she pulled out her hard brush and brushed her hair into a ponytail. Once her ponytail was secured, she twisted her hair into a ball and secured it with another ponytail holder. After making sure her hair was straight, she then put on eyeliner and some clear lip gloss. After that, she put on her diamond studs and TTC chain. Then she went to dress in her TTC gear, saving her gun holster and 9mm for last. Liam watched her from the doorway of the bathroom, still clad in his towel, as she did all of this.

"Nigga, would you get yo' ass dressed and hurry up? We ain't got time fo' yo' pretty boy routine either," London spat when she caught him ogling her.

"You gon' quit with this pretty boy shit cause ain't nun pretty about me and ain't nothing fo' damn sure pretty about my D game, that shit a beast. I'ma MONSTER on dat pussy," he replied, quoting some Future's Monster lyrics as he walked to where his clothes laid on the floor and began picking them up and putting them on.

Once he was finished getting dressed, tool and all, he went over to London's vanity mirror, picked up her hard brush, and stooped down so he could see himself in the mirror. Then he began brushing his smooth, dark brown waves.

"Man, if you don't bring yo pretty ass on," London spat.

"Shut up. You know yo' ass happy that you finally got this pretty nigga's dick."

London tilted her head to the side. "If I remember correctly, it was you that hemmed me up against the wall and tried to fuck my brains out."

"Ah, but it was you in the car kissin' all on a brutha, getting' shit started," Liam replied as he pulled her into his arms, close to his body. She looked up into his eyes and then

98

smirked.

"Well you kept pestering me, asking why I was being so mean to you and that was my way of giving you an answer," she responded softly.

"Well shiid, if that's how yo ass respond to being pestered, then I'm 'bout to lock us in a room and see what yo' response is like after being interrogated and badgered with questions."

London chuckled at Liam's remark. "You dumb as shit, you know that?" she said as she broke their embrace.

"You love my dumb ass."

"Whhaatteevvvaaa," London responded as she started walking in the direction of the door, making sure everything was turned off in the process. London was at the door when Liam pulled her backwards into his body and wrapped his arms around her.

"Liam, qquuiitt. We gotta go."

"I know but you ain't even bout to get off tryna play me to the left like that, shawdy. I ain't dumb by far and I know yo ass love me whether you admit it or not. It's in ya face, it's in ya walk, it's in ya voice, it's in your moan when you screaming out my name when I'm deep in my pussy," he spat as he cupped her center. "Now say you love me and we will leave," he spoke in a soft voice next to her ear.

"Liiaamm," London whined. She hated admitting her feelings to anyone including herself. Truth be told, she fell head over heels the first moment she laid eyes on him.

"Admit it. Admit you love me and we can leave," Liam said then stuck out the tip of his tongue and traced the edge of her earlobe with his tongue.

"Alright, you're right. Now let's go."

"Right about what? Say it out loud. Don't be scared, shawdy."

"Okay, okay, you're right, Liam. I do love you and that's what scares me. I have never loved a man, not even my own daddy. Now come on, bae, we gotta go," London spat.

Liam let go of her, slowly making a mental note to discuss this with her at a later date. Right about now they did have to go.

They stepped outside into the warm summer night ready to shed blood. Gone was the soft lovey dovey shit, which had now been replaced with some real killer shit. They hopped in Liam's car and sped off. Their destination was the west side of Charlotte, the hood. Liam cranked up Jeezy's new song Holy Ghost and bobbed his head to the music.

Fifteen minutes later, they were pulling up to some apartments called Little Rock. Liam kept his eyes peeled for his cousin, hoping to spot him or his girl out and about in the neighborhood. It was his lucky day. His fam was still hanging outside.

"Aye yo, Drew. Drew," he yelled out the window trying to get his little cousin's attention. Drew turned his head in the direction of where he heard his name being called and spotted Liam's blacked out charger sitting on 22's.

"Whud up, big cuz?" Drew hollered out as he approached the driver's side of the vehicle.

"Nun much. Say man, you heard anybody talkin' smack about kidnapping some kids, beefing with Yaseer?"

"Naw, not that I can think of."

"What about anybody new in town in the same business as us?"

Drew took a minute to ponder the question. "Come to think of it, it's this new crew showing up on the blocks bit by bit."

"Name, Drew, I need names."

"Uh, uh," Drew stuttered before coming up with a name. "Oh yea, they call themselves TKC for The Killa Crew. They not from 'round here though. I think they come out of ATL. Um, I know it was this chick I had smashed like two weeks ago, her name was A—Adele, Adelene, Akayla, something like that. Hell, I'on remember. Alls I know is her pussy."

"Adela?"

"Yeah. Yeah, that's her name. Shawdy was thick. Big ass, small waist, nice breast size, long hair, and she was pecan brown, wwwooo shawty was bad. Any who, she a part of that TKC crew from what she told me."

Liam frowned his face at the thought of Adela, the woman he knew was just thick all the way around, no curves or nothing, just straight up big boned with a streak of gray hair in the front of the hair that she always kept in a bun. His face frowned even more at the thought of a crew trying to jock there style by calling themselves The Killa Crew. Da fuck, Liam thought to himself.

"A'ight fam, that's what it do. Here ya go, my ninja," Liam said as he handed him a big face.

"Oh yea, Drew, you betta stop fuckin these hoes. Re-Re gon' kick yo ass if she catch you cheatin' on her," Liam spat with a smile as he put his car into to gear, cranked his music, and pulled off.

Liam activated his hands free car phone. "Call Yaseer," Liam requested, getting his wish immediately. Drew watched Liam's tail lights and said a small prayer that his cousins would be safe.

Chapter 17

Copycat

"Whud up?" Yaseer answered as he stepped out of ear range of a sleeping Paris.

"Aye bruh, we got a TTC copycat."

"A copycat, what the fuck you mean a copycat?"

"It meant exactly what the fuck I said, nigga. We got a fuckin copycat. Man you ain't gone believe this shit. Where you at? I'm 'bout to come scoop you up fo' a sec so I can give you da scoop, bruh."

"I'm at the hospital with Paris. Call me when you get near so I can be outside waiting on ya," Yaseer spat then disconnected the call. He turned around and walked over to Paris' bedside.

"What's going on Yaseer? And don't tell me nothing."

"P, you need to be resting and I don't need you stressing over something that you can't do nothing about."

"I'ma stress more if ya don't tell me."

Yaseer knew she wasn't lying about that. Not knowing would just bug her even more. He ran a hand over his breath and exhaled.

"Look ma, long story short, the twins are missing.

Adela helped in their kidnapping, and now we have a crew that is apparently biting our style. There is more. I'm waiting on Liam to get here and give me the rundown."

"What?" Paris screamed as she attempted to get out of the bed.

"Paris! Paris!" Yaseer called out, trying to get her attention. "Paris," he called out in a raised voice.

Paris stopped moving immediately, knowing that when Yaseer raised his voice that really meant he was in no mood to play games. He hardly raised his voice and when he did he truly meant business.

"Look ma, all I need you to do is rest ya body and take care of my seeds. Let me and the crew handle this situation. We got this," Yaseer said to Paris as he caressed her face with his thumb.

"Ok bae, but please keep me posted."

"I will, bae. Now get some rest. I'll be here when you wake up in the morning."

"Ok, bae," Paris responded in a soft voice as she lay back down in the bed and covered herself back up. Before she knew it, she was dozing off.

Yaseer sat watching Paris sleep until his phone started vibrating. He knew it was Liam calling to let him know that he was almost to the hospital. Yaseer got up out of the chair beside Paris' bed, kissed her on the cheek, and made his way down to the main entrance of the hospital. He saw Liam pulling up as soon as he was walking out. Liam stopped right in front of him. London got out to climb into the back seat. She looked Yaseer up and down with major attitude as she got in the backseat.

"Hey to you too, London," he spat.

"Hey," London grunted out dryly with a roll of her neck.

"Aye L, we need to have a talk."

"Uuhh, no we don't. We ain't got shit to talk about unless it concerns murkin' somebody. Otherwise, I ain't got no holla fo' ya, shawdy," London replied with major attitude.

Yaseer bit his tongue as he got in the car. There was no way in hell he was about to take that disrespect from anybody, let alone a female. The only reason he didn't check her right then was because they were in front of the hospital and he didn't want to cause a scene, but he was definitely going to check that ass though.

Liam was in the driver's seat seething because London was really showing her ass. Once Yaseer had put his seatbelt on, he pulled off. They had been driving for a little over ten minutes with Liam giving him the rundown of what Drew had told him. They had just turned down a long dark road that was surrounded by nothing but trees when Yaseer told Liam to pull over to the side of the road. Liam looked at him sideways but did as his big brother requested and pulled over to a dirt area of the road. Yaseer got out and opened London's door.

"Step out the car fo' a moment, lil' momma."

She looked at him sideways then went back to checking her Facebook page on her phone. Yaseer looked to his left, and then his right. He knew she just didn't flat out disrespect him like he was a random nigga off the street. Yaseer snatched her phone out of her hand and tossed it in the street, causing it to shatter into pieces.

London's bottom jaw dropped. She couldn't believe that he had really just broken her phone. Her face turned red as a beet and she all but lost it. She jumped out of the car faster than lightning and was all up in Yaseer's grill ready to punch his lights out. She may be a bitch, but she was no bitch, and she was not scared of Yaseer, or nobody else for that matter, not one bit.

Liam looked on in shock, knowing things were about to get crazy dumb in 2.9 seconds. He didn't know who to defend, his woman or his brother. Liam got out of the car praying he could calm their headstrong asses down.

"Da fuck wrong wit yo stupid ass," London yelled in

106

Yaseer's face as she mushed him in his head.

Liam stopped in his tracks. Oh shit, he thought to himself knowing that Yaseer was about to flip the fuck out. Liam had told her at the house to cool the fuck out so he was about to let her take her medicine. She needed to realize who the boss was, who she worked for, and that she didn't run shit. So instead of approaching them, he leaned against his truck and lit a blunt.

Yaseer grabbed London and pushed her into the car catching her off guard. Then he got in her face.

"Don't you ever in your life put yo' muhfuckin' hands on me again. I promise if ya do, it will be the last movement your hands ever make," he spat in an eerie calm voice. "Let that be the last time you disrespect me. If you feeling salty wit me, then air that shit out so we can get it straight cause I will be damn if I got another muhfucka on my crew aiming fo' my head silently. Do you understand me?"

London nodded her head up and down in response.

"Now that we got that out the way, please explain what the fuck yo' beef is wit me so we can cook that shit up and eat it."

London went on to tell him the same thing she had vented to Liam about earlier. Yaseer listened intently to her concerns and actually understood her anger because, knowing

107

him, he would be pissed too.

"Look shawdy, I'm grown so I can admit that I was wrong for the way I handled shit between me and P earlier. That was my B and I admit that, but I won't apologize for being pissed at the bullshit she withheld from me. No matter what, she should have told me the moment she found out. Now as for the other problem you addressed, it was not my intent to not call you. It was so much going on that I honestly forgot. My mindset was and is on killing the muhfuckas who got my seeds, as well as anybody else who was involved in my kid's kidnapping, along with whoever was responsible for carrying out Ezra's last wishes by making sure I received that DVD, knowing it would fuck my world up. Now with that being said, let's go find one of the fools involved so we can do what we do best, torture 'em," Yaseer responded. Then he patted her on the shoulder and got in the car.

Chapter 18

Unexpected

London got back in the car happy that her beef with Yaseer was somewhat resolved, but now her anger had been shifted in another direction, to the driver of the vehicle, Liam. She stared a hole in the back of his head, thinking he could have at least tried to come to her defense instead of standing there looking stupid and smoking on some loud.

Liam looked at her in the rearview mirror as if he could sense her vibes and shook his head as if to say I told you so. London looked at him for a split second before averting her gaze, feeling a little guilty for showing her ass.

"Uumm, Yaseer…" she called out softly.

"Yea, sis?"

"Umm, about my phone, I'ma need a new one. Ya kinda broke my other one."

Yaseer looked over his shoulder, smiled, and shook his head.

"A'ight, I got you, shawdy. That one was outdated anyway," Yaseer replied with a slight chuckle.

London was a trip but he had mad love for her like she was his own flesh and blood. Liam pulled back onto the road and busted a U-turn to take Yaseer back to hospital.

"Aye Liam, get with Kai'Yan and Zyon to see if they found out anything, and let me know. Paris is supposed to get released in the morning. London, I need you to take her to your house until I purchase a new one. I can't have unknowns knowing where me, my girl, and unborn seeds rest our heads at," Yaseer stated as they pulled up at the hospital's main entrance.

"I'ma get with y'all in the morning. Be ready to go full force starting in the morning."

"I'ight," Liam said as Yaseer shut the door.

London made movement to get in the front and Liam shook his head.

"Stay yo' ass right back there. Yo' ass is in time out for that shit you pulled."

"Time out?" London questioned with her face scrunched up.

"Hell yea, yo ass is in time the fuck out," he said as he pulled off.

"Whateva... If yo ass wanna be my chauffeur and drive me around like you driving Ms. Daisy, then that's fine by me. By all means, please do so."

Liam stopped at a stop sign before exiting the hospital parking lot. Again, he shook his head.

"Don't even try it, shawdy. That reverse psychology

110

shit ain't even 'bout to work on me."

London crossed her arms, with her lips pouted and slouched down in the seat. She couldn't believe she was being treated like a five-year-old.

*****

"Stop pouting like a five-year-old, gull. I'm 'bout to go get you some hot wings," Kai'yan stated as he got out of bed preparing to throw some clothes on to go get Brooklyn some wings. He just wanted an hour of sleep. He had been searching non-stop for the information that Yaseer had requested.

Needless to say, it did not go exactly as he had planned it to. Their name ran deep in the streets and put fear in the hearts of those young and old, well at least the young and old who thought ill of them. But a lot of young and old respected them for at least giving back to the community. TTC's body count was ridiculous. They could literally fill a whole cemetery with all of the bodies they had accumulated just in the previous year alone.

Kai'yan wasn't even planning on that number tonight, but there was no way he was about to let two fools who were a part of some wannabe TTC talk slick to him. So he popped the bump that their brains sat in like a pimple. All they had to do was answer two simple questions: who sent them and what were they doing in the Carolinas. Instead of answering the questions, they started with all the smart talk, not even knowing the beast they were coming up against. Now they couldn't answer shit or go back to tell anyone anything.

Kai'yan sort of respected them for at least not snitching. But one thing their boss should know was real niggas didn't keep their name a mystery. They sent niggas proudly boasting their name. Real bosses didn't hide behind their workers. They got out with their workers and did the dirty work with them. Everybody knew him and felt him but whoever the cat was that was putting this new crew on the block had to be more of a pussy than puss in boots.

"Thank yyooouuu," Brooklyn sang out in a happy sing song voice, ecstatic that she was getting her wish. Kai'yan had just laced up his J's when he heard his phone start going off. No one but the crew called this late. He adjusted his sweats, walked over to the nightstand where his phone was, and answered it.

'Whud up, fam," he answered in a baritone voice.

"A lot, bruh, you found out sum?"

"Yea, I found out who dem plates belong to and went to track some info down, which led me to some fake wanna be TTC that ended up with me having to pop a couple

112

pimples open," he answered, referring to the incident with him killing the two guys.

"Damn. Aye listen, I'm on the way to your house now. I'm 'bout to come scoop you up right quick so we can discuss our findings."

"Cool," Kai'yan responded before disconnecting the call.

"Everything alright, bae?" Brooklyn questioned with concern laced in her face.

"Yea ma, everything Gucci so relax yo' trigga finga, shawdy," he replied causing Brooklyn to smile at his remark. He knew she stayed ready to body a dude like a trained assassin. Pregnant and all, she would still put someone on their back at the drop of a dime.

"A'ight bae, don't make me have to pull my ratchet out cause you know I will."

"Don't I know it," he responded with a smirk. "Alright love, I'll be back," Kai'yan said as he walked out of the room to the door.

Kai'yan walked into the dark living room to grab his wallet off the table. Something didn't feel right. Kai'yan pulled his tool discreetly just to be on the safe side. He bent over and grabbed his wallet off the table and slid it in his pocket. He straightened his pants and ran a hand over his shirt preparing to go outside to wait on Liam.

Pow! A shot rang out.

Kai'yan spun around with his tool in the air aiming for his mark only to see he had it pointed at a very pregnant Brooklyn who was also holding a gun. He heard a moan and looked down on the floor to see a masked man rolling about on the floor holding his butt cheek. Kai'yan looked back up at his girl and then back down at dude. He lifted his size thirteen and commenced to stomping dude for even having the audacity to come in his girl's house, let alone pull a tool on him. He flung his dreads back after he delivered the unknown man one last kick to his ribs. Then walked over and flicked the light switch to the living room.

Chapter 19

Frozen

Beep! Beep! Liam beeped the horn for Kai'yan to come out. Kai'yan opened the door and signaled for Liam to come in. Liam parked his car figuring it really must be important for Kai'yan to request him to come in knowing that they were supposed to be getting ready to ride so they could talk about their findings. Liam got out of the car, followed by London. They walked up to the open door in silence. Liam looked at her one good time, silently telling her to not to be on no bullshit.

Liam and London walked into the house and were greeted by both a pissed off looking Brooklyn and Kai'yan. The couple turned and walked in the direction of the living room followed by London and Liam with befuddled looks on their faces.

"Yo, y'all good?" Liam questioned.

"Yea, we good, but he's not," Kai'yan said as they turned the corner of the living room.

"Da fuck happened?"

"I was out here getting my wallet about to come outside to wait on you. I had a feeling something was off. The atmosphere just didn't feel right. I can't really explain it. Next thing I know, I hear a shot ring out. I turned around ready to blast off and there ya sister was holding her piece and this nigga was on the floor rolling and moaning like a bitch clasping his butt cheeks. Speaking of ya sister," Kai'yan paused for a second as he turned to face Brooklyn. "What in the world was you doing out the room and how in the hell you knew to have that thang ready to sound off?" he questioned.

Brooklyn frowned her face up for a split second before answering his questions. "First off, you know my ratchet stay ready to sound off. Second, I was coming out here to catch you to tell you to bring me back some cookies and cream ice cream along with my hot wings. When I stepped out the door, I saw somebody behind you with their tool aimed at ya head so I quietly reached over and slightly slid the top drawer on the black dresser open. I felt for my piece that I had under all my panties, pulled it out, and shot him in the butt cheek. I started to shoot him in the head, but thought about the fact that the bullet could go through and hit you. Then I aimed at his chest but the thought came to my head to not kill him just yet. What fun would it be if we couldn't torture him? So I chose to shoot him in the butt cheek. That shit's gonna hurt like hell to sit on," Brooklyn concluded with a sinister smirk. At that moment, Kai'yan realized she was just as crazy as her eldest brother, if not crazier.

"Well damn," Liam said kind of shocked. He knew his sister didn't mind busting one off, but hell, she literally just saved her man's life, literally. And the crazy thing was shawdy really seemed to enjoy it. He shook his head. Then he looked over at the idiot lying down on the floor and his anger spiked.

Liam walked over to where the guy laid on the floor and picked him up by the collar of his shirt. Dude couldn't have weighed more than a buck fifty. Liam quietly carried the lightweight John Doe to the car, without saying anything to anyone, and threw him in the trunk like it was nothing. He just got into the driver's seat of his car and looked at the threesome standing on the porch like they didn't know what was up. He leaned his head to the side and looked at them like they were stupid.

Catching Liam's drift, they locked up the house and got into the car with Liam, already knowing their destination and what was about to go down. Liam once again activated his hands free car phone and commanded it to call Zyon.

"Yo," Zyon answered on his Bluetooth.

"I need you to go get Yaseer from the hospital."

"I know whatever it is can't be good if y'all wanting

me to scoop him up at damn near three in the morning on a Sunday."

"Yeah it is. You know that song 187 by the Davis' ain't no joke shawdy."

"Aw shit, a'ight let me go scoop 'em up. We will meet y'all at the doctor's office in the waiting room," Zyon responded, referring to the Chambers.

Liam disconnected the call, and then looked over at Kai'yan.

"You hit Yaseer up yet?"

"Yeah, I just texted him hot one letting him know what was up."

"Cool," Liam replied, and then turned the music up.

Thirty minutes later, they were pulling up at The Chambers. They all climbed out of the car and went to the trunk that Liam had just popped. They all frowned their faces at the foul order.

"Eeeww my nigga, did you really shit on yourself?" London questioned, holding her nose.

"Yous a nasty mudda sucka," Kai'yan spat as he stepped back a little.

Just then they saw headlights pulling into the parking lot. They turned to see Zyon and Yaseer pulling up behind them. Yaseer got out of the car with a fierce mug on his face

118

that clearly stated he was not in the mood for the bullshit. This was his second time being pulled away from Paris, plus he was still on fire about his daughters being missing and about Adela. He was beyond ready to kill up something.

"Da fuck is that smell?" Yaseer questioned as they got close up on the car.

"This pussy ass nigga done shitted on his damn self."

"Damn, what the fuck did yo' ass eat? That shit stank. Damn," Yaseer said as he shook his head at the stench.

"Aye Zy, you carrying him," Liam spat.

"Nigga, fuck you. Yo' ass carrying him," Zyon replied, looking at Liam like he had him fucked up.

"Would both of y'all shut the fuck up bickering like lil' bitches. Move out the damn way," Yaseer ordered.

They moved out of the way to let an angry Yaseer walk through. Yaseer raised his hand and pimp smacked his next victim across the face, causing dude eyes to pop open with fear. Yaseer picked his new victim up by the throat, lifted him up out of the trunk, and placed the guy's feet on the ground.

"You better move them feet and walk the best you can."

They all walked to the entrance of the chambers with their victim in tow. Yaseer still had his hand around the guy's throat. Yaseer used his free hand to punch in the code to get inside of The Chambers.

Once they were in, they bypassed the waiting room and went straight to the room where they planned to kill their victim. Once they entered the room, Yaseer put the guy inside of a white porcelain tub. It sort of looked like one of the old-school tubs you would see in the movies, except there were spots with straps attached to them. One of the straps was at the top of the tub, it was a connecting strap. It was made that way so that when a person's hands were pulled above their head, it could hold on to both of the person's wrists. Then there were two straps inside the tub to hold a person's ankles in place. The straps were made out of genuine leather. They were truly built Ford tough.

Yaseer strapped the guy to the tub and snatched off the young man's ski mask.

"Why were you in my sister's house?"

"To fuck ha, hoe ass nigga."

Yaseer pulled a switchblade out of his pocket and swiped it across the guy's chest, cutting him deep enough to draw blood but not deep enough to kill him.

"Uuummm," John Doe grunted out in between clenched teeth. Between the bullet in his butt and the cut on his chest, he wished he could just die because the pain was starting to become unbearable. If telling the man who had just cut him what he wanted to know would help get him out of this situation, rather it was by getting set free or death, then so be it. It was what it was.

"Now I'ma ask you again. Why the fuck were you at my little sister's house?"

"Look man, if I tell you what you want, will you let me go?" John Doe groaned out in pain.

"Yeah man, I'll let you go. Just answer my questions and we can get this over with."

"A'ight listen, I was supposed to come there and murk shawdy. That's all I was told. I ain't know nobody else was going to be in there. I was told she lived alone. They gave me the address and I just want to do what I was paid to do."

"Okay, next question. Who sent you?"

"This woman named Adela."

The fuck is up wit this fuckin' woman, Yaseer thought to himself. He couldn't figure out for the life of him why she had an aught against him. Maybe he had killed someone she knew or something. But even with that, she still had major balls coming for him. He needed to get in contact with his dad as soon as possible. She hadn't even been in the Carolinas long enough for him to even kill someone she knew. It had to be something else and he was bound and determined to find out what it was.

"A'ight lil' buddy cuz, thanks for the info," Yaseer said as he turned to walk away. He stopped and looked over his shoulder. "Ice em," was the only command Yaseer gave before he continued walking to exit the room.

"Hey. Hey, I thought you said you was going to let me go," John Doe yelled out.

"I am letting you go... letting you go straight to hell," Yaseer spat over his shoulder as he opened the door and left out of the room.

Kai'yan went to a deep freezer that was stationed in the corner of the room and got two big bags of ice out. He walked back over to the tub, took out his own switch blade, and cut the bag open.

Everyone in the crew except Brooklyn, due to her condition, mimicked the very thing that Kai'yan had just done. They all grabbed two bags of ice, took them over to the tub, and cut them open. Kai'yan was the first to pour ice over their victim.

"Noooo man, noooo. Y'all ain't gotta do this. Come on, man, let me go," John Doe pleaded on deaf ears. The rest of the crew followed his lead and poured their bags of ice over their victim.

Once they were done pouring their bags of ice on him,

Liam walked over to a big metal door that sat in the back of the room, punched a code in, and opened the door. It was one big freezer. He held it open as Kai'yan and Zyon pushed the tub, along with their victim, into the ice room.

Brooklyn grabbed a plastic bag out of the cabinet on the wall, walked over to London, and handed her the bag. She took the plastic bag out of Brooklyn's hand, walked into the freezer and placed the bag over a pleading John Doe's head. She didn't even bother to tape the bottom of it around his neck because there was no way he could get it off being that his hands and feet were tied up.

After they made sure he was secure, they all walked out of the room and Liam moved his foot out of the door's way so that it would close. They watched as the door closed and automatically locked, successfully locking their victim inside.

"Damn," Liam muttered.

"What?" London questioned.

"That was cold as shit," Liam said with a smile on his face. The crew had to chuckle at his shenanigans.

"Yo' dumb ass would say something like that," Zyon spat.

"Shut up, nicca, you act like it would kill yo' ass to fuckin' crack a smile," Liam said as they exited the room.

Now they had a whole new mission, somewhat, and that was finding Adela.

Chapter 20

Vanished

It was one and a half weeks later and it seemed as though Adela had vanished into thin air. Yaseer was getting madder and madder by the moment. He was hoping and praying no one had gotten to her fat ass before him. Yaseer was stressed to the max. His twins were still missing and he had no clues as to where they could be. The only person that could lead him to them was Adela and now she was missing.

On top of that, the trip to see his Dad just made things even worse. Come to find out after having a conversation with his dad, the Adela his dad recommended and had sent was NOT the Adela that showed up at his house. In fact, from his dad's description, she was the total opposite. The real Adela was dark skinned, in her late 40's not early 60's, and had a little weight on her but not as much as the Adela that had showed up at his house. Also, the real Adela was around five-foot three inches tall. The Adela that showed up at his house was at least five-foot eight or five-foot nine. And last but not least, the real Adela had a short haircut but the Adela that showed up at his house had long hair.

Yaseer didn't know what the fuck was going on. And

after finding out his granddaughters were missing, Yaseer Sr. was just as heated, if not more because of the fact it was only so much that he could do from behind bars. Yaseer's mind was in overdrive as he rode alone with just his thoughts, August Alsina crooning in the background with the dark surrounding the outside atmosphere. He let the lyrics sink into his soul.

But if I don't make it home tonight/ Take some money to my sister/ I don't ever want her chasing after niggas/ 'cause where I'm from, niggas outchea dying every day/ And they ain't all bad/ they just tryna make it/ And I ain't no different/ So if I get missing/ These are my last wishes/ I hope you get them right/ Girl, if I don't make it home tonight.

Yaseer used his free hand to reach into the secret compartment of his arm rest to grab a blunt and his lighter. He put the blunt in his mouth and lit it, letting the exotic trees relax his troubled mind so that he could think of his next move. Preferably his best move.

Yaseer sang along with August, feeling as though August was singing about his life and speaking on how Yaseer felt every time he stepped out the door of his home.

"I know it's harsh, but this how I feel. Girl, it's coming from the heart, I hope it doesn't end the way it had to start 'cause it started out bad but I made it this far. But everyone ain't tryna see me make it, or they only wanna see me make it so they can take it 'cause I know it's hard to find a job so niggas kill and rob. There's a chance that I won't make it here tomorrow…"

A lone tear escaped. And for the first time, Yaseer let the tear leave its mark at the edge of his chin. He was getting tired of the game. He was getting tired of putting his family and friends at risk. He was ready to just settle down with Paris and his kids and literally just enjoy life. He had more than enough money to last them the rest of their lives. The more he thought about it, the more he loved the idea. He was just as sure that the crew would probably like the idea, too. They had to be tired of the bullshit, too. Who wouldn't be?

He made up in his mind that once they found the girls that would be the next plan they set into motion. If the crew wanted to keep going, they could and he would appoint someone in his place. But as for him and Paris, they were done.

Yaseer pulled up at one of his traps on Milton Rd. His antennas shot up when he pulled up and saw a brawl about to go down in front of the spot. He put the roach of his blunt in the ashtray, grabbed his piece and the silencer to it, and then jumped out of the car. These have to be some of the biggest fools I have ever met, he thought to himself.

"Fuck yo' boss, ain't nobody scared of that pussy nigga," he heard one guy say.

"Pussy? Nigga, yo' boss the pussy. What boss tries to copy another man's swag by making up a copycat crew? Fuck outta here, nigga can't even purchase his own ideas. Now who the pussy nigga?" he heard another say.

"My boss was smart enough to fuck Yaseer's world up with his bitch ass. Watch my crew murk y'all niggas one by one. Starting with yo bitch ass first," dude said as he began to pull his tool.

Everything got silent as Yaseer's workers noticed him approaching. Yaseer put his index finger over his mouth silently telling them to remain quiet as he walked up on his next toe tag. Yaseer walked up looking suave in his TTC gear, making it appear as if he was an ordinary street hustler just with higher rank. Yaseer walked up beside the guy and began a conversation like he had been there the whole time.

"What up, lil' buddy cuz?" he greeted the guy who had been talking ill about him and TTC.

"Ain't shit up. Who da fuck is you?" he said turning to Yaseer, mugging, not even knowing the danger he was in.

Yaseer smiled showing off a beautiful set of pearly whites. "Who am I? I'on know, shawdy. You tell me since you know so much about me."

"I see you just as dumb as these lil' fuckas. Nigga, if I asked who the fuck you were that means I don't know you," he spat slowly as if Yaseer was slow, and then turned to the guy he had with him and started laughing and dapping him up.

Yaseer smiled along with them like the joke was really funny. When in actuality he was laughing at their stupidity of talking about somebody they had never even met face to face. Then all of a sudden, his smile disappeared just as fast as it came. Yaseer balled his fist and punched dude in his stomach, causing dude to bend over, clutching his stomach and trying to catch his breath. His boy went to grab his piece and was shot in the head before he could even get it out.

Yaseer bent down to where dude was still bent over clutching his stomach and asked in a low voice. "Still think I'ma a pussy?"

Yaseer took the guy by the collar and dragged him to the traphouse, practically throwing him inside. Yaseer took off his crisp black tee and laid it on the couch so he wouldn't get it wrinkled. His victim spit blood out on the floor.

"Dog, I'on even know who da fuck you is, but if you rockin' wit dese TTC niggas, then hell yeah you a pussy," he spat.

Yaseer picked ole boy up off the floor, stood him on

his feet, and then took his booted foot and kicked him across the room knocking furniture over in the process.

"Fool, I own this crew. I'm that nigga you was calling a pussy. I'm the boss, nigga. I-run-these-streets-muhfucka," Yaseer spat in between kicks to the guy's side. Yaseer bent down and pulled dude's head up by his raggedy dreads so that he could see his face. "That's right, nigga, I'm Yaseer. Next time, before ya start runnin yo' mouth make sure you know who the fuck you speaking on or at least what the fuck they look like. Now what was that hot shit you spit about ya punk ass boss fuckin' up my world, son?" Yaseer questioned with venom laced with every word.

"Fuck you," dude muttered in a barely audible voice. Yaseer bobbed his head up and down.

"Um hmm, that's what you say now. We gon' see how you feel in about two hours. Cake, come tie this nigga up and throw him in my trunk," Yaseer ordered one of his hustlers.

Cake was a tall, muscular guy that was the color of smooth dark chocolate. He rocked a low haircut with three hundred sixty degree waves. Yaseer had nicknamed him Cake because when he first met him that's exactly what he was doing, getting cake any kind of way, selling any and everything. He sort of reminded Yaseer of himself when he first started. At the command of Yaseer, Cake grabbed the dude off of the floor, tied him up, and began following Yaseer to his car with dude tossed over his shoulder. Yaseer stopped at the door and backed up a little, turning his gaze on a cat named Jay, the man he had put in charge of this particular trap spot who was now seated at the table.

"How the argument get started?"

"I'on even know, Boss. I was in here handling this lil' nigga Desert cause he came up in the trap short for a third damn time."

Yaseer nodded his head up and down as he pulled his tool from its holster and screwed the silencer on it.

"How long ago them fools arrived and started talking smack in front of my trap?" he questioned.

"About six minutes before you arrived," replied Jay.

Yaseer nodded his head up and down once more, taking in Jay's responses. "Now when you heard the commotion, you didn't think you could have postponed handling lil' man until after you got them idiots from in front of my trap causing a scene and drawing attention?"

"Naw, I thought getting money was more important than handling a stupid argument," Jay answered.

"One more question. Why did Desert still have any breath in his body after coming up short a second time? Better yet, why the fuck is he still breathing now?" Yaseer

131

asked as he turned his attention to Desert and shot him in the head.

Jay watched with his mouth opened wide as his lil' brother's body fell to the floor.

"Now you say they had been out there going at it about six minutes before my arrival?"

Jay nodded his head up and down silently as he began to feel hatred in his heart for the man that just took his brother's life, as well as a wave of sadness because his brother would have never been killed if he hadn't even gotten him involved in the life of fast cash.

"Stand up fo' me right quick, Jay. I need to thank you."

Jay followed Yaseer's orders, as usual.

Yaseer aimed his gun at Jay's left kneecap and let his tool speak silently as it removed Jay's knee cap. Then he moved his hand swiftly and shot out his other knee cap. Jay let out a loud yelp at the immense pain he felt as he fell to the floor, no longer able to stand on his own two feet.

Yaseer walked over to where Jay had fallen on his side beside the table and was trying his hardest to belly crawl away. Yaseer once again aimed his weapon and shot Jay in both his left and right hands.

"Aaaahhhhhh," Jay screamed out. He thought about

132

pleading his case, but already knew where he had messed up at and automatically knew he was a goner. Plus, he refused to go out begging like a hoe. So he laid there awaiting his final moments and repenting to God for the sins he had committed on earth.

"I wanna thank you personally for showing me that you are not the correct G to run my trap. Now that's four shots so far. A shot for every minute you let these idiots cause more and more of a commotion in front of my trap, making it hot for everyone in here, putting everyone at risk. Two more minutes to go. Hhhmmm, where shall I aim next?" Yaseer asked himself. Then he aimed his gun one more time and blew out Jay's last thoughts with two shots to the back of his head.

"Aye Tool, get my black tee from over there on the couch," he ordered one of his workers.

Tool moved swiftly, not wanting to be the next person on Yaseer's hit list. Yaseer took his black tee and slid it over his head, and then smoothed it in place once he had it on. He looked at everyone in the house and his eyes landed on the guy that had been arguing with the guy that Cake was still holding over his shoulder.

"Next time a nigga start coming at you like a bitch, don't argue with 'em, just blow his brains out. It's as simple as one two three, see," Yaseer said as he

raised his gun one last time and shot him between the eyes. "Clear this spot out and burn it," Yaseer spat on his way out the door with Cake behind him and his next victim on tow. Yaseer pressed the button on his key to pop the trunk to his all-black charger. He went and got into the front seat as his package was deposited in the back.

"Aye Cake," Yaseer called out as he leaned out the driver's seat with his eyes fixed on the back of the car. Cake shut the trunk and walked around to Yaseer's driver's side.

"Yeah Bossman."

"You in charge of this trap now. I need you to move all the dope and gwap out of there and fire that shit up. Don't leave no evidence. I need you to find a new spot to stash my shit and trap out of. Can you handle that?" Yaseer questioned.

"Yeah, I can."

"Cool, don't fuck up," Yaseer warned. Then he shut his car door, turned his car on, plugged his phone up, and tuned on Mike Will's Buy the World, turning it up almost to the max. He pulled off bobbing his head to the music. After he had been driving for about ten minutes, he turned the music down and dialed Liam's number.

"Yo," Liam answered.

"You at da house?"

"Yeah, I just got here. Was up?" Liam questioned.

"You fed Joshua and Sampson yet?" Yaseer questioned about his two massive pit bull dogs that Liam had been keeping for him while he was in his coma and continued keeping until Yaseer felt he was ready for them to come back to the house.

"I'm actually fixing their bowls now."

"Don't feed them."

"Oookkaayy, any specific reason."

"Yeah, I'm on the way to get them, to scoop you, too. We got some shit to handle. I'll be there in ten minutes. I'm on Independence now."

"A'ight, see ya in a few"

"A'ight," Yaseer said as he disconnected the call and turned his music back up.

Chapter 21

Chow

Yaseer pulled up at Liam's house no less than ten minutes later and beeped the horn. Liam came out with both of Yaseer's pits on their leashes. Liam opened the backdoor to Yaseer's car so the dogs could get in.

"Sit," Yaseer commanded, and the dogs obeyed. Liam closed the back door and then opened the passenger door and got in. Once Yaseer saw Liam put his seatbelt on, he put the car in gear and pulled off.

"Aye, text Kai'yan, London, and Zyon 187."

Liam nodded his understanding and texted the crew letting them know what was about to go down. They automatically knew to come to The Chambers when they saw that text.

About twenty minutes later, Yaseer was on the dark back road that he had driven numerous times over and over headed to The Chambers to add another ghost to the collection of ghosts that were already there. He pulled into the parking lot, parked the car, and hopped out ready to do damage. His crew was pulling up right behind him. They unloaded their next victim and carried him inside of The

Chamber's with the dogs in tow.

They carried him down the hall to room number six. When they opened the door, it almost looked like a kitchen, Stove, refrigerator, counter, table and all. However, as with all of the other rooms in The Chamber, there was a specific spot for their victim to be strapped down. In this particular room, it just so happened that the straps were in various spots on the table. The table was adjustable so that it was able to accommodate any person's height.

"Get 'em strapped," Yaseer ordered as he pulled a black chair that was seated beside the counter. He stationed the chair next to where his victim's head would be and sat down in it. He pulled out a bag of blueberry Kush and a cigarillo and proceeded to gut the cigar and roll up a blunt. Once he was finished rolling the blunt, he sat it on his lap. He watched as they secured the last strap on the table and then stood back to admire their handy work. Yaseer put the blunt between his lips and replaced the bag of weed in his sweats. He got up and walked over to the other side of the counter, opened the drawer, and pulled out a blowtorch that looked similar to the ones used to light coal on a grill.

He walked back over to his victim, who looked pissed off that he was even there in the first place, but at the same time looked frightened as to what was about to go on.

"Still think I'm a pussy?" Yaseer questioned with a sinister smile on his face. "Bet that boss of yours ain't never seen no shit like this."

"Nigga, please, we got one just like this in the A, so yep I still think yous a straight pussy," dude spat.

Yaseer's anger rose one hundred degrees. Who the fuck had the balls enough to even try to jack TTC's swag? However, he did not let his inner turmoil show on his face. Yaseer nodded his head up and down as he took the blow torch, lit it up, and then took the tip of the blunt and lit it. He turned the blow torch off and then turned to face his victim.

"I'm going to ask you some questions. Answer them and I may be lenient, fuck with me and I will make your final moments a living hell," Yaseer threatened.

"I ain't answering shit for none of y'all bitches. Y'all can suck my dick," dude replied.

Yaseer didn't even respond. He passed the blunt to Liam, starting the rotation. Then he went back to the drawer that he had gotten the torch from, pulled out a piece of paper, and walked over to the refrigerator and pulled out a bottle of water.

Yaseer walked back over to where they had the guy chained down. He put the bottle of water on the counter and held the piece of paper up in the air, lit the tip, and watched it burn a little before he placed the flaming paper on his victims crouch. Then he sat back in his chair.

"Aaahhhh. Aahhh. Okay. Okay. I'm sorry. I'm sorry. Move it. Move it. I'll answer your questions," dude screamed.

Yaseer waited for a few seconds before he got up and got the bottle of water off of the counter. He unscrewed the cap and poured the water over the fire that he had started. The stench of burnt clothes and flesh filled the air.

"Glad to know that you're ready to cooperate. Now who is your boss?"

"His name is Juice, him and his moms run the crew."

"Okay, where are they stationed? What's the address?" Yaseer questioned.

"They live in Atlanta. I'on know the exact address though."

"What part of Atlanta?"

"Buckhead, but they got a spot over in Bankhead, too."

Yaseer nodded his head up and down as he took in the information.

"One last question. You said your boss fucked my world up. Elaborate on that for me."

Dude exhaled. He couldn't believe he was snitching,

139

something he swore up and down that he would never do.

"Look, all I know is they were trying to take out anybody close to you, including your daughters, ya girl, and ya siblings too," dude answered.

Again, Yaseer nodded his head up and down at the information that he had just received.

"Thanks for the info. I got some light work to handle. Lower the table," Yaseer ordered as he got up and walked to the door. He opened the door and his pit bulls that he had stationed outside the door walked in.

"Come on y'all, we got work to do," he told the crew.

The crew started heading to the door, exiting out the door that Yaseer held open. He was the last one to leave out. Before he closed the door, he gave one final command. "Eat." He heard his dogs begin to growl and attack their meal as his victim screamed for dear life.

"Aye Kai'yan, hit up the cleanup crew to clean the remains of old dude and to put the dogs to sleep."

"Put the dog's to sleep?" Kai'yan questioned, knowing how much Yaseer loved the animals.

"Yes. They have tasted human blood. Ain't no turning back after that. I don't need them attacking me or anyone else close to me. So they have to go," Yaseer replied.

Kai'yan nodded his understanding and did as Yaseer

had requested. The crew walked out quietly not having much to say, each in their own thoughts.

Yaseer's mind was on his precious girls and Paris. He shook his head at the eerie thought of anyone taking away his loved ones. Ironically, that was something he did everyday but was something he didn't want done to him. He vowed to himself that after they got his girls back, he was getting out of the game. He was going to re-up one last time, sell that, and be done with it. He was giving himself six months to get out for good and possibly move away.

Chapter 22

Baby, Baby, Baby

"Listen up," Yaseer spoke getting everyone's attention. "Kai'yan, I need you to use your connections and find out who this nigga Juice is and get an exact address. Matter of fact, tell the cleanup crew to keep ole buddy's phone. I got an idea. Umm, London, I need you to go get Paris and y'all both go up to Kai'yan's. I don't want neither one of y'all females out and about. Stay there until I call for y'all. If anything happens, let me know. Don't leave that house unless someone goes into labor, then get to the hospital as soon as possible. Other than that, stay put."

London nodded her head quietly as her brain went into overdrive. She was worried about everyone. She, too, was starting to think that she didn't want to live this type of life anymore. She was a certified medical assistant and could get a job working in a doctor's office and put this part of her life behind her. It was cool for a while, but she had outgrown it. London got in her car and pulled off, leaving the crew behind.

"Liam, follow her to get Paris then follow them up to the Kai'yan's ranch to make sure they get there safely,"

Yaseer requested in a low voice.

"Got ya, big bro. Don't worry, we gon get 'em. We always do," Liam stated with a small smile as he got in his car and sped off to catch up to London.

London rode to her house in silence, seriously thinking her life over. She looked in her rearview mirror to change lanes and noticed Liam tailing her. She smiled and shook her head. Yaseer would have Liam be the one to follow her. Her panties got soaked just thinking of Liam's hands all over her body as she stared into his dark green eyes. He did something to her body every time without even having to lay a finger on her.

She switched lanes so that she could get off at the exit that led to her house off of Albemarle Rd. Before she knew it, they were pulling up at her house. Liam pulled in behind her and parked his car. He smacked her plump butt as he walked past her to her front door. He took out the key that she had given him and unlocked the door with London on his heels.

"Help. Someone help me." They heard Paris crying out. Liam broke into a sprint to the living room. Paris was on her hands and knees on the floor.

"Paris," London screeched out as she ran to her sister's aid. "Are you ok?" she asked in a concerned voice.

Paris shook her head side to side signaling that she

was not alright.

"Babies. Bleeding. Hurting. Hospital. Now!" Paris said in between pants.

London looked down and saw a big red spot on Paris's grey sweat pants and broke into a panic. "Liam. Liam, pick her up. Come on, we gotta go we gotta get her to the hospital now," London yelled frantically.

Liam scooped Paris up into his arms and carried her to his car. "Open the back door, L."

London opened the back door to Liam's charger so that he could put Paris in the car. Then she rushed to the other side of the back seat so she could keep an eye on her. She climbed in beside Paris, put Paris' head on her lap, and rubbed her hair as Liam pulled out and sped to the hospital, getting them there in less than ten minutes.

He pulled up at the doors of the emergency part of the hospital, parked his car and hopped out to get Paris. He picked her up in his arms and carried her inside, screaming help the whole way.

Paris was beginning to lose consciousness and Liam was beyond scared, as was London, who was right on his heels, as usual. A nurse came running out of the triage department to see what was going on. When she saw Paris' head tilted back not giving a response and Paris' belly along with the blood on the front of Paris pants, she broke into a run to help.

"I need a doctor down here, stat. Bring me a stretcher. I need one now," she yelled.

Another nurse came running with a doctor and stretcher in tow. The doctor immediately took Paris out of Liam's arms and placed her on the stretcher.

"Come on, let's move. Move! She needs to get to Labor and Delivery now," the Doctor yelled.

Liam and London moved along with the doctor and nurses, trying to see if Paris was going to be okay.

"Y'all are going to have to wait in the waiting room," the nurse ordered, stopping Liam and London in their tracks.

They watched as the doctor's loaded onto the elevator with Paris and silently prayed that she would be alright.

"We gotta call Yaseer," Liam said in a soft voice as he took his phone out and made the dreaded call.

"Y'all almost at Kai'yan's?" Yaseer asked as he turned the music down in his car.

"Yaseer..." Liam paused to get his words together.

"What Liam? Whatever it is, spit it out. We ain't got time to waste. We got shit to do."

"Paris is in the hospital. They are taking her up to Labor and Delivery as we speak," Liam waited on Yaseer to respond. "Yaseer, Yaseer," he called out in vain. Liam took his phone from his ear only to see his screensaver. Yaseer had hung up. Liam looked over to a tear stricken London and pulled her into his arms.

"It's gon' be okay, boo. You know P a fighter. Her and my nephews are going to be just fine," he said, trying to sooth her worries.

London cried in his arms, hoping that he was right, hoping and praying that her sister would be alright. Liam guided London to the elevator and got on to go up to Labor and Delivery to sit in the waiting room and wait to hear something from the doctors. London and Liam sat in silence hoping for the best.

Their heads popped up at the sound of footsteps. They looked up to see a gloomy looking Yaseer walking into the room. He sat down across from them in silence for a few minutes before saying anything.

"It seems like everything is hitting at fuckin' once. My daughters, Paris and our unborns, the stuff with TTC, it's too damn much. I'on know how to tell y'all this but to just say it. Once I get my girls back, I'm done. I can't do this shit no more. My body is tired. I can't keep going through the bullshit. For once, I just want to live in peace. After I get my girls, we gon' re-up one last time. Now if y'all wanna keep

146

going, go ahead. But as for me and Paris, no more, we are through," Yaseer stated as he leaned his head back on the chair.

"On the real tip, I feel ya, bruh. I been thinkin' 'bout that shit too, but it's like what I'ma do afterwards. The street life is all I know."

"I feel ya too bro-in-law but honestly this shit ain't fo' me no more either. I think I'm 'bout to let my tool R.I.P.," London chimed in.

Everybody sat in their own worlds just thinking about life. They were in their own zones when they heard footsteps. All of their heads popped up to see the doctor walking into the room. Yaseer jumped to his feet, followed by London.

"Is my fiancé and unborns okay?" Yaseer questioned in a worried voice.

"Yes, she got here just in time. Her blood pressure was elevated again, and more than likely it was due to the contractions she was having. However, we did have to do an emergency C-section because the babies were in distress. They are doing fine just as well. It looks like we may have been off with the timing though. The babies' weight is consistent with thirty two weeks, which means Paris was a little over six months pregnant. They are very strong, though. They will have to stay in the NICU, Neonatal Intensive Care

Unit, at least a month to gain a little more weight. Right now they are a little over three pounds."

"And Paris? Is, is she alright?" Yaseer questioned.

"Yes she is in a stable condition. She is sleeping right now," the doctor responded.

Yaseer let out the breath that he had been holding. He was more than relieved that his heart and his seeds were okay.

"Can I see them?"

"Yes, you can," the Doctor said as he turned and began to lead the way with Yaseer, London and Liam following him.

They walked for what seemed liked forever to the NICU. Once there, they each had to wash their hands for thirty seconds before going back to see the twins. Yaseer followed the doctor to the babies. His breath caught in his throat seeing the beautiful creations that he and Paris had made. He was more than sure that the babies were his. They looked just like him, with

a hint of Paris in each of their features.

For a moment, Yaseer forgot all the trouble that was going on in his life. It was remarkable to see a life that you helped create. He looked in the incubator with a renewed hope that everything was going to be alright. Now he was more than determined to handle his business and be done.

Yaseer scooted to the side so that London and Liam could get a look at the babies.

London looked at her nephews in awe, silently hoping one day that she too would be blessed to be a mother. Liam looked on in awe as well. His eyes shifted to London as she looked down at the two precious gifts who were sleeping their lives away. In some strange way, he could feel her yearning. She just didn't know what he had in store for her. He planned to make her his wife one day and implant her with his seed. And if things worked out like he wanted them to, then it would be sooner than later.

Liam looked away from London and caught Yaseer eyeing him with a silly smirk on his face. Yaseer shook his head side to side. He knew something was going to pop off between Liam and London, he just didn't realize it had already popped off until now. He was happy for the two, and he was sure Paris would be too.

Chapter 23

Parenthood

"A'ight y'all, I'm 'bout to go check on Paris," Yaseer said as he began walking toward the exit.

"I'm coming, to," London followed.

"Me three," Liam chimed in.

They all made their way to the room that Paris had been admitted to. Yaseer knocked before walking in. She was still asleep. Yaseer walked over to her bed and stared down at her angelic face. She had truly been through a lot with him and still gave birth to his seeds. His love grew for her ten times more. The rest of the anger that he had for her from keeping the secret about her father suddenly vanished as if the slate had been wiped clean. He bent over and kissed her plush lips. He stood back up to his full height. As much as he hated to he had to leave and go take care of business. He needed to get his girls back. He wouldn't be whole until they were back.

"Hey y'all, I'm 'bout to dip. Paris is resting and the twins are asleep as well. I need to handle this situation before my girl and son's come home," Yaseer stated hoping they would understand. "Oh and Liam, I need you to go check on Brooklyn before we head out to the A."

"To the A?" Liam questioned.

"Yep. It's a wonder what people keep on their phones," Yaseer said with a smirk as he made his way to the door.

Liam watched his big brother, thinking that he was truly one of a kind. London walked over to her big sister's bed, bent over, and gave her a kiss on the cheek before standing back up. She went to turn around to leave and bumped into Liam. His arms wrapped around her waist and held her tightly.

"And just where do you think you're going, Ms. Lady?" Liam asked and then lightly pecked her on her lips.

"To help Yaseer get the girls back."

Liam was shaking his head before she even finished her statement. "No, you need to stay here with your sister. We will get the girls back."

"Liam, Paris will never forgive me if something was to happen to Yaseer."

"Nothing is going to happen to Yaseer, bae. Come on now, he got his two brothers and best friend watching his back. If anything, one of us will get hurt before him."

"That's even more of a reason for me to go. I can't let nothing happen to you or them."

Liam laughed and tapped her lightly on her bottom.

151

"I know you love a nigga and all, but yo ass still can't go. Stay here with your sister. We will be back love," Liam replied. Then he kissed her once more, deepening the kiss and pulling her closer.

"Hhmm, you betta stop for I bust dat open again before I leave," Liam said in between kisses.

London's response was to wrap her arms around his neck and pull him closer.

"Would you two get a room?" They heard someone whisper in a groggy voice.

They broke apart immediately, embarrassed about getting caught kissing and groping each other. London turned around to see her big sister's sleep filled eyes open and looking at them with a smirk on her face.

"Whatever," London said with a huge grin on her face as she rushed over and gave her sister a big hug. "Omg, you scared the shit out of me. Don't you ever do that again," London spat with a pout.

"It wasn't intentional, I promise."

"When are you going to name my nephews?" London questioned.

Paris looked down at her belly in shock. She didn't even realize she was no longer pregnant.

"Where's my babies? Are they okay? Oh gosh, how

could I have not realized I had them?" Paris shot out questions frantically.

"First off, you had all types of medicine in your system. Second, you was asleep. Third, them babies are just fine. They just gotta get their weight up. And oh yeah, they need a name besides baby A and baby B," London answered.

Paris relaxed after hearing London's response. "I need to see them first before I name them. I already have their names picked out. I just got to see which name fits who the best. I know one will be named Ja'seer Elijah and the other one's name will be Na'Seer Elysha," Paris answered, then let out a yawn.

"I feel ya sis, well get some rest then hopefully they will take you to see the twins," London replied, kissed her sister on the forehead, and prepared to go down to the cafeteria to see if they had anything good to eat.

"K" was Paris' only response before she drifted back off to sleep.

"I'm about to go see what the Cafe has to offer. Keep me updated on what's going on," London said as she made her way to the door. She went to open the door when a masculine hand moved faster than hers to open it for her. London looked back over her shoulder at Liam looking down at her with a smoldering look in his eyes.

"Let me find out you're a gentlemen."

"Baby, I been one. You just been sleeping on me."

"Now baby, you know I never sleep when I'm on ya," London teased and then walked out of the door.

"Keep talking that hot shit and I'ma tap that ass," Liam said as he exited behind her.

"Oh please do, baby, please tap all of this ass," London replied.

"What you hungry for?" Liam questioned, ignoring her last remark on purpose.

"I really want some hot wings but at the same time I want some fettuccini alfredo."

"Okay, well come on let's go get something to eat and go check on Brooklyn. Then I will drop you back off on my way to meet Yaseer."

"Cool," London said as they arrived at the elevator. They stepped onto the elevator without saying a word to one another. Liam stood close to London as they watched the doors close. London reached over and pressed the number one to go down to the main lobby. As soon as the elevator started moving, Liam reached over and pressed the red button to stop the elevator from moving.

"Liam," was the only thing that she could get out before his lips were on hers.

154

He lifted her leg by her thigh and began a slow grind. His hand reached in between the waistband of her black jeans and panties. He moved his index and middle fingers back and forth on her womanly pearl causing her to moan out. His finger slipped between her womanly folds, moving in and out of her sex. It took less than two minutes before she was squirting on his fingers.

Liam broke their embrace and pressed the button to finish there descend to the main floor. London fixed her clothes and looked at Liam. She couldn't even decide rather she wanted to be mad at him for not finishing what he had started or not. All she knew for sure was that food was the last thing she wanted. Right about now, she wanted the man who had her insides all hot and bothered. The doors of the elevator opened and Liam looked back at London with his hand extended as if nothing had just happened with his megawatt smile on full blast.

"Come on, dearie," he requested.

She took his hand and obliged his request. She couldn't help but to smile as well. They walked outside hand in hand, each lost in their own lustful thoughts.

Liam escorted her to his car and opened the door for her. Once she settled in good, he shut the door then went and got in on his side. An hour later, they were pulling up to

Kai'yan's ranch with food in tow. London had decided on getting some wings from Zaxby's. They got out of the car, went up to Kai'yan's, and rang the doorbell. Brooklyn opened the door with a pint of banana pudding ice cream.

"Hey, hey, hey, what you two doing out here in the boonies?" she questioned.

"I see Kai'yan nor Yaseer has told you anything," Liam said as he walked in, followed by London.

"Told me what?"

Liam let out a deep breath.

"We found out who has the twins and where they reside. Oh and Paris went into labor early and they had to do an emergency C-section but she and the twins are doing just fine now. Did I miss anything?" he asked looking at London.

"Nope," she shook her head signaling that he had not.

"Wow, I can't wait to drop this load so I can get back in the loop. I hate not being able to be there like I need and want to be. And dammit, how the hell Paris ass go in labor before me? Hell, my ass is pushing damn near nine months," Brooklyn questioned with a smile. She was more than anxious to see her newborn nephews.

"We came to scoop you up. We need you to be with London and Paris while we are out of town."

"Out of town? Where the hell y'all going?" she questioned feeling upset that she was finding out at the last minute that they were leaving.

"We going to Atlanta to get the twins and murk the idiot that has them."

Brooklyn nodded her head up and down in understanding.

"Well alright then, let me grab my things and we can go," Brooklyn said as she went to her room to grab her purse along with her .9mm. "Alright, let's go," she said as she came back out.

"Hold on, sissy pooh, let me use the restroom right quick"

"Go on, sis, take your time, that gives me time to finish this last bit of ice cream and grab me some snacks to take with me," Brooklyn replied to London as she went into the kitchen. London excused herself to the ladies room so she could tinkle before they made the long ride back to Presbyterian Hospital.

Chapter 24

Quickie

Liam looked to make sure his sister was still busy in the kitchen then snuck off in the direction that London had just walked in. She had just made it to the bathroom and was about to shut the door when Liam stuck his foot out to block the door from closing.

London opened the door and looked at him like he had lost his mind.

"Liam, go on now. I gotta pee."

"And so you shall, now move before we get caught," Liam spat.

London moved back to allow him entrance into the bathroom. Then she locked the door behind him. As soon as she turned around, Liam was on her like white on rice. He grabbed her by the waist and pulled her to him with his lips landing on hers. The sexual energy passing between them was so strong that it would break them both in half if neither of them got the satisfaction that they both longed for.

London suddenly forgot about emptying her bladder. That became the last thing on her mind as

Liam unbuttoned his and her pants. He let them fall to the ground as he pushed her jeans over her plump bottom and down her legs. London used her foot to pull them and her shoes off all the way.

Liam lifted her and sat her on the edge of the counter. He entered her slowly until he was to the hilt. He began moving in and out of her at a slow pace, gradually picking up speed. London gripped Liam's shoulders as tightly as she could, feeling like she was about to die because it felt so good. Liam removed his lips from hers only to have them trail down to the side of her neck beneath the edge of her chin, causing her to moan out. Liam pulled his lips back slightly.

"Sshhh," he said trying to quiet her down to keep from getting caught.

The pace to his thrusts increased. He picked her up off of the counter and turned her back to the nearest wall behind them.

"Uuumm, aw shit, you feel so good, baby," he spat as he pumped harder, enjoying the feel of her tight walls wrapped around his manhood.

"Mmm, mmm, fuck me, Liam. Harder, baby, harder," she cried out.

Liam angled himself to where he knew he would hit her G-spot just right and began working that area overtime to bring them both some relief.

"I'm cuumminngg," London moaned out in pleasure. That was only added gasoline on to the fire for Liam. He slowed his pump into a slow grind knowing that would set her off.

"Fucckk," she swore at what he was doing to her body. "Aw shit," she swore once more as her body began to spasm and her slippery walls became soaked and started gushing like a faucet.

Liam increased his pace, pumping faster and faster as he felt his nut teetering on the edge. London brought her lips to his neck and let her tongue out to play. That was all it took for Liam to burst off deep inside her womb. Liam held her hips tight to keep them still as he emptied that last bit of his seed inside of her before pulling out of her and placing her feet on the cool white tile. He kissed her lips one last time before pulling away from her to fix his clothes.

"You so nasty," London cracked as she picked up her jeans and put them back on.

"Don't blame me, it's all yo fault. Every time I come around you, I can't keep my hands to myself or control my damn hormones."

"Let me find out," London said as she washed her hands and opened the bathroom door.

"You just did," Liam said as he smacked her ass walk-

160

ing past her out the bathroom.

"Got damn, it took y'all long enough to nut," Brooklyn cracked.

"You can't rush good lovin'," was Liam's comeback.

London's face turned beet red as she slapped him on the shoulder.

"What? I'm just being honest."

"Well bring yo' honest ass on, we got to go," London responded walking to the door.

Brooklyn and Liam followed behind her making sure everything was turned off in the process. They exited the house, piled into the car, and began their journey back to the hospital. It was halfway through the ride that London remembered she had to pee. She could have slapped Liam because now she had to wait until they got to the bathroom. She refused to pee in a restaurant bathroom. It was just something about it that wouldn't let her do it. She laid her head back on the headrest thinking that it was well worth the wait.

Chapter 25

Black Out

Liam watched as London jumped out of the car and ran to the bathroom like she was on fire. He got out to help Brooklyn out of the car then watched to make sure she made it into the hospital okay before jumping back in his car, putting it in drive, and going to meet Yaseer, Kai'yan and Zyon.

Fifteen minutes later, he pulled up to Zyon's condo and hopped out to go meet them. Liam knocked on the door and waited for one of them to open it. Zyon opened the door with his tool in hand ready to blast off, but lowered his gun when he saw who was at the door. He stepped back to let his little brother enter.

"What up, big bruh?" Liam asked as he walked past Zyon.

"Ain't shit, just getting suited up to go catch these idiots and get our nieces back."

"True. Did Yaseer bring extra weapons with him?" Liam questioned ready to go to war with whomever.

"You know big bruh brought them thangs,"

Zyon replied as they walked to the back room in the condo where Yaseer and Kai'yan where both suited up in black cargo pants, black t-shirts with black bullet proof vest on top, topped off with black Timbs and their guns on their waists in their holsters. They truly looked like they were ready for war and they truly were. Yaseer would move heaven and earth for his children and the crew would do the same. Yaseer threw Liam a black bag that contained some black cargo's a bullet proof vest and extra weapons.

"Strap up, lover boy, time to bust them thangs," Yaseer spat.

"Hell yea," was Liam's reply, letting the lover boy comment roll off his back. They didn't have time to go back and forth. Play time was over. It was time to get down to the nitty gritty and put some people six feet under the dirt.

"A'ight, so listen up. I went through ole boy phone and found both a number for Adela, as well as that nigga Juice. I hit them up telling them it was a major problem with the work that they had sent to be put out on the streets. I also have them thinking that Brooklyn and Kai'yan are both dead. So right now they probably think I'm over here depressed and crying. One last thing, I talked them into coming down here. I paid a few disgruntled cats in their crew off to bring them down to A1. So instead of going to the big A, we going to our version of the A, our own personal party."

"Now that's what the fuck I'm talking about," Zyon

said, dapping Yaseer up.

"Hell yea," Kai'yan chimed in, dapping Liam up. They were more than ready to greet their guests, who were definitely not expecting them.

*****

The parking lot was full at A1.

"Seer, how the fuck we gon' get these fools without harming no one else?" Kai'yan questioned.

"You will see. Trust and believe everything is not what it seems," he replied, leaving it at that.

Yaseer parked at the back of his club and hopped out more than ready to take someone's soul like he was born the grim reaper. The crew followed his lead and went through the back door of the club that led to his office. He walked into his office, went to the TV he had hanging on the wall, took the remote off the top, and turned the TV on. He had the TV hooked up to the camera system so he could keep an eye on everything that was going down while he was not on the floor. It looked as though everyone was enjoying the party. Drinks were flowing, music pumping, and people were at the bar ordering wings to go along with their drinks. Yaseer's eyes scanned the monitor until he found his targets.

"You see her?" He pointed to the screen.

164

They nodded their heads, taking in the attractive lady on the screen.

"Yeah, who is she?" Liam questioned, looking at her and trying to figure out where he knew her familiar face from.

"You don't recognize the woman who knocked dat ass out?" Yaseer questioned with a grin.

Liam went a little closer to the screen and looked at it with a little more concentration.

"Oh, my fu— Oh, my damn. Adela," Liam spat as he turned around to face Yaseer with a shocked expression on his face.

"The one and only," Yaseer replied enjoying the look on his little brother's face. He, too, had been shocked when he saw what Adela truly looked like.

The guys he had paid off had showed Yaseer Adela's Facebook page.

Facebook pages can get you in some trouble you ain't even ready for, was the thought that ran through Yaseer's head when he was browsing through her Facebook.

"Now this nigga, Juice, I have no clue as to what he looks like besides him being tall and light skin. So just keep yo' eye's peeled open," Yaseer replied as he walked over to his desk and sat down.

"We will go down there in about ten minutes and get this show on the road." No less than ten minutes later, the crew was heading to the V.I.P. section where Adela was sitting, enjoying a bottle of Moscato as she played on her phone, not even paying attention to her surroundings. The DJ turned on Migos *Freak No More* when he saw Yaseer approaching Adela. Adela was still in her own little zone, not having a clue as to what was going on.

"Excuse me, beautiful. Would you like to dance?"

"Nah, I'm good," Adela said as she continued scrolling through her newsfeed on Facebook.

"Come on, lil' momma, just one dance."

If it was one thing that Adela couldn't stand, it was a grown man calling her lil' momma or shawdy. That was one of her pet peeves. She popped her head up ready to go off on the man who obviously couldn't take a hint. Her words caught in her throat. She couldn't believe her eyes. Adela looked into the eyes of a man she was told was dead.

Kai'yan looked down at Adela with a smirk on his face then dropped his hand and moved over to let Yaseer through. Yaseer held up his hand to signal the DJ to stop the music.

"Well, hello there, Adela, or should I say Ms. Carmichael, Jillian Carmichael to be exact."

166

Jillian looked at him with all the hate she felt in her heart for him.

"Boooyyy, don't you look like a brand new woman. Gone is the grey streak, the dark make-up, and oh yeah the extra weight. Damn, Weight Watchers been on their shit, or nah? I bet it feel good as hell to have that hot ass fat suit off, huh? You had my ass fooled. Hell, you had us all fooled."

"Fuck you, nigga. You know who the fuck you even talking to or dealing wit, son," she spat back.

"Ooohh, look at that, even the southern drawl is gone. Is that a New York accent I hear? Ah, don't even bothering answering that. I already know. I tell ya, boy, that Facebook will get you in trouble every damn time," Yaseer spat, amused at his own comics. "Now that that's out the way, where the fuck are my daughters, you psychotic bitch?"

"Wouldn't you like to know?" she replied with a sinister smile as she sat back with her arms folded across her chest. Yaseer nodded his head up and down, something he did very often when he was about to do something crazy or was taking in need-to-know information. Yaseer glanced off to the side, and then with swiftness pulled his .22 and shot her in the shoulder.

"Listen you old ass hoe, I ain't got time to play with yo' silly ass. I'll blast yo' shit to kingdom come and still find out where my daughters are at. Ain't a man or woman alive that can stop me from finding them," Yaseer spat.

"Guess you better get to blasting then, but before ya do, take a closer look at this old ass hoe. Come on now, you don't recognize your big cousin's face? Getting clean off of crack does wonders for a person and so does a little nose job."

Yaseer peered at her closely and shook his head in disbelief. She was supposed to be locked up.

"Still don't recognize me all the way? Look over your shoulder. You recognize him?" Yaseer looked over his shoulder and damn near had a heart attack at the sight. This couldn't be. The man he was looking at was dead. He knew he was because he had killed him himself. Hell, the whole crew had killed him.

"Ezra," he heard Liam mutter.

"Scary, huh? Meet Ezra's twin brother Eli, also known as Juice. Now look back at me."

Yaseer's head slowly turned back to her face.

"Now meet their momma. You honestly thought a prison could keep me from getting to you after you killed my son? Umm umm, baby, you gots to pay for that. Juice, get him," she commanded.

Juice lifted his pistol to shoot Yaseer. All of a sudden,

blood and brain matter flew out the front of Juice's head. His body crumpled to the ground and there was London with her gun still pointed. Yaseer went to turn his head back to Jillian and was met with the business end of her .45.

"Nooooo," was the last word Yaseer heard as two final shots rang out in A1, leaving everyone stunned.

To Be Continued...

Boss'N Up 3: Heart of the Streetz

Coming Soon

ACKNOWLEDGMENTS

Ding! Ding! Ding! Back in the ring for round 2! Looks like she's in it to win it! Miss Royal Nniiccoollee!!! LOL Just messing around. Any who this is the second go around for me and yes I'm in it to win it, well win the hearts of my readers that is. I'm going to try to make this as short as possible. If I forget a name charge it to my brain and not my heart, loves.

Now let's officially get this started! First off I want to thank God for giving me the talent to write! Without him I am nothing
.
LDP WHAT'S POPPIN MY HITTAS!!!! (Singing My Hittas by YG)

I said that I'ma ride for my mfn hitta
Most likely I'ma die with my finger on the trigger
I've been grinding outside all day with my hittas
And I ain't goin in unless I'm with my hittas
My hitta, my hitta...
(Sorry y'all I was over here jamming let us proceed...)

Cash the Boss man aka Mean man LOL (Jp) I want to THANK YOU for giving me the opportunity to live a dream that I didn't even think was possible. Thanks to you for giving me the shot that turned my dream into reality. Much Love, Boss Man.

Latisha Lewinson. Thank you for all that you have done. Whether it was to give advice, be my shoulder to cry on, or lend a helping hand, thank you for that and much more. You are truly a blessing. Love ya, big sis!

Frank Gresham. My mo-fo ninja!!! I rocks with you the long way. Thanks for the advice and laughs you have given me during my good and bad times. You are truly a friend indeed as well as you are truly appreciated! Much love to you!

Forever Redd. CAROLINAS STAND UP! Hhheeyyy, shawdy! Omg the countless hours we have spent on the phone talking about our dreams, goals, and everything else under the sun is always worth it! Thank you for lending an ear or advice when I needed it. You are a remarkable woman!

Tranay Adams. (Singing) Going up on a Tuesday, got ya girl in the club and she choosing. LMMAO just playing around with ya. You always laugh at my corny ish LOL. Thanks for being a good friend! Much Love.

Coffee. Ayyeee What's Up, Miss Nola? How you doing? (Wendy Williams Voice) Thank you! Thank you! Thank you! There's so much I could say but none of it sums it up more than those two words. Love you lots and again Thank you!

Linnea. All I'ma say is I'ma need Stone and Krissett to have a happy ending please and thank yyoouuu LMMFAO! Keep blazin' that pen! Much Love, hun!

Lenika. OMG! You so petty. Stop drinking that dang milk Tish sent you! It makes you lose your butt not gain, she lied to you LOL LMBO JK. Thank you for all of your love and support and for being who you are. You are the best! Love ya, sis!

Jpeach Jpeach. My Ace boon koon! That purple though! Theyon' know about it! Yo pen game some serious, girl! Keep pushing it! Much Love!

LadyStiletto. Hhheeyyy, booski! You are a doll! I can't wait to read that hot ish you spitting on them keys!

Mahaughani and Kanari Diamond. I have not had the chance to speak to you ladies much but hopefully we will talk soon! I can't wait to read you work. Much love to you both!

Teddy Duke and Askari. Welcome to the family can't wait to read your work!

Sharon Bell, Sandy, Momma Jane, Bigmofrmbfflo, Authoress Anoshi, Nicky Earl, Rita Smith, Norma Jacox Wade, Bernie Bagley, Sabrina Eubanks, NeNe Capri, Mrs.Lissha, Mrs.Toni Doe, and Marie A Norfleet Thank you all for your love and support. Y'all are the best!

Kenya Anthony. Thank you for everything you have ever done and your support.

MasterPiece and Giles. I love y'all! Thanks for rocking with me the long way through the good and the bad!

Cristana Kelsey. YOU MY MOFO NINJA LOL!!! No other words needed!

Damion King. What's up 2 names! Thanks for everything! Much Love to ya!

Alright now let's get ready to wrap this up with me thanking my Carolina rounds!

Courtney, Crystal, Koren, Lia, Sher'Nee, Rosco, Sade, Evelyn, Kasey, Ma Denise (Keep having programs and I will keep dancing LOL) The Sargents, Kasey (Love you sweets, thanks for your love and support in everything!) David, Koren and Kay Kay, thank you for all of the love and support you have ever shown I truly appreciate it. Whether it was to beat up your eardrums, wet your shoulders with my tears or to help me and mine with whatever we needed, Thank you! Lia go on and do that documentary white I mean black girl LOL LMAO CTFU! Love ya, sissy pooh!

Christa and Lina. What's good, baby mommas? LOL I love y'all to pieces. I rocks with y'all the long way and ain't nothing that can change that. Smooches!

To Aunt Vikki, Mani, Kayla, Mikey, Lee Lee, Lo Lo, and Ma Dukes I love y'all more than words can explain! Thank you for being there for me from the time I was little until up until now and the future. You all have literally become my family. Blood couldn't make us any closer. Once again, thank you for all you have done and do I love you!

David Clark. Thanks for keeping me happy and the smiles you put on my face. You're the best. Thanks for all that you do my love!

To my siblings Gene, Kia, Onjie, Shameer, Andrew, and Aaron Love y'all!

To my nieces and nephews (To many of you all to name LOL) Auntie Loves y'all!

To my Parents Trascy Grady, Eugene H. Davis II, and Jeanette Davis, I Love Y'all.

To my cousins, aunts, and uncles much love to you all!

Last but not least to my angel, my princess, the reason I

grind, Neriah Krissett Dunlap!!! MOMMY LOVES YOU WITH ALL OF MY HEART!!! We gone make it, baby girl. We gon make it! Love you, momma's girl!

Again to anyone I may have missed charge it to my brain and not my heart. Love you all very very much! I hope you enjoy Boss'N Up 2: The Naked Truth just as much as you enjoyed Boss'N Up part 1! *Toodles*

Stay Connected with Us!

Text **LOCKDOWN** to 22828 to
stay up-to-date with new releases,
sneak peaks, contests and more...

Thank you!

Submission Guideline.

Submit the first three chapters of your completed manuscript to ldpsubmissions@gmail.com, subject line: Your book's title. The manuscript must be in a .doc file and sent as an attachment. Document should be in Times New Roman, double spaced and in size 12 font. Also, provide your synopsis and full contact information. If sending multiple submissions, they must each be in a separate email.

Have a story but no way to send it electronically? You can still submit to LDP/Ca$h Presents. Send in the first three chapters, written or typed, of your completed manuscript to:

LDP: Submissions Dept
Po Box 870494
Mesquite, Tx 75187

DO NOT send original manuscript. Must be a duplicate.

Provide your synopsis and a cover letter containing your full contact information.

Thanks for considering LDP and Ca$h Presents.

Coming Soon from Lock Down Publications/Ca$h

Presents

BOW DOWN TO MY GANGSTA

By **Ca$h**

TORN BETWEEN TWO

By **Coffee**

BLOOD STAINS OF A SHOTTA **III**

By **Jamaica**

WHEN THE STREETS CLAP BACK **II**

By **Jibril Williams**

STEADY MOBBIN

By **Marcellus Allen**

BLOOD OF A BOSS **V**

By **Askari**

BRIDE OF A HUSTLA **III**

By **Destiny Skai**

WHEN A GOOD GIRL GOES BAD **II**

By **Adrienne**

THE HEART OF A GANGSTA **III**

By **Jerry Jackson**

LOYAL TO THE GAME **IV**

By **T.J. & Jelissa**

A DOPEBOY'S PRAYER **II**

By **Eddie "Wolf" Lee**

IF LOVING YOU IS WRONG... **III**

Royal Nicole

LOVE ME EVEN WHEN IT HURTS

By **Jelissa**

DAUGHTERS SAVAGE

By **Chris Green**

BLOODY COMMAS **III**

SKI MASK CARTEL II

By **T.J. Edwards**

TRAPHOUSE KING

By **Hood Rich**

BLAST FOR ME **II**

RAISED AS A GOON V

BRED BY THE SLUMS

By **Ghost**

A DISTINGUISHED THUG STOLE MY HEART **III**

By **Meesha**

ADDICTIED TO THE DRAMA **II**

By **Jamila Mathis**

LIPSTICK KILLAH II

By **Mimi**

THE BOSSMAN'S DAUGHTERS 4

WHAT BAD BITCHES DO

By **Aryanna**

Available Now

RESTRAINING ORDER **I & II**

By **CA$H & Coffee**

LOVE KNOWS NO BOUNDARIES **I II & III**

Boss'N Up 2

By **Coffee**

RAISED AS A GOON I, II, III & IV

By **Ghost**

LAY IT DOWN **I & II**

LAST OF A DYING BREED

BLOOD STAINS OF A SHOTTA I & II

By **Jamaica**

LOYAL TO THE GAME

LOYAL TO THE GAME II

LOYAL TO THE GAME III

By **TJ & Jelissa**

BLOODY COMMAS I & II

SKI MASK CARTEL

By **T.J. Edwards**

IF LOVING HIM IS WRONG...I & II

By **Jelissa**

WHEN THE STREETS CLAP BACK

By **Jibril Williams**

A DISTINGUISHED THUG STOLE MY HEART I & II

By **Meesha**

PUSH IT TO THE LIMIT

By **Bre' Hayes**

BLOOD OF A BOSS **I, II, III & IV**

By **Askari**

THE STREETS BLEED MURDER **I, II & III**

THE HEART OF A GANGSTA I & II

By **Jerry Jackson**

Royal Nicole

CUM FOR ME

CUM FOR ME 2

CUM FOR ME 3

An **LDP Erotica Collaboration**

BRIDE OF A HUSTLA **I & II**

THE FETTI GIRLS **I, II& III**

By **Destiny Skai**

WHEN A GOOD GIRL GOES BAD

By **Adrienne**

A GANGSTER'S REVENGE **I II III & IV**

THE BOSS MAN'S DAUGHTERS

THE BOSS MAN'S DAUGHTERS II

THE BOSSMAN'S DAUGHTERS III

A SAVAGE LOVE **I & II**

BAE BELONGS TO ME

A HUSTLER'S DECEIT I, II

By **Aryanna**

A KINGPIN'S AMBITON

A KINGPIN'S AMBITION **II**

I MURDER FOR THE DOUGH

By **Ambitious**

TRUE SAVAGE

TRUE SAVAGE II

TRUE SAVAGE **III**

By **Chris Green**

A DOPEBOY'S PRAYER

By **Eddie "Wolf" Lee**

THE KING CARTEL **I, II & III**

By **Frank Gresham**

THESE NIGGAS AIN'T LOYAL **I, II & III**

By **Nikki Tee**

GANGSTA SHYT **I II &III**

By **CATO**

THE ULTIMATE BETRAYAL

By **Phoenix**

BOSS'N UP **I , II & III**

By **Royal Nicole**

I LOVE YOU TO DEATH

By Destiny J

I RIDE FOR MY HITTA

I STILL RIDE FOR MY HITTA

By **Misty Holt**

LOVE & CHASIN' PAPER

By **Qay Crockett**

TO DIE IN VAIN

By **ASAD**

BROOKLYN HUSTLAZ

By **Boogsy Morina**

BROOKLYN ON LOCK I & II

By **Sonovia**

GANGSTA CITY

By **Teddy Duke**

A DRUG KING AND HIS DIAMOND

A DOPEMAN'S RICHES

Royal Nicole

By Nicole Goosby

BOOKS BY LDP'S CEO, CA$H

TRUST IN NO MAN

TRUST IN NO MAN 2

TRUST IN NO MAN 3

BONDED BY BLOOD

SHORTY GOT A THUG

THUGS CRY

THUGS CRY 2

THUGS CRY 3

TRUST NO BITCH

TRUST NO BITCH 2

TRUST NO BITCH 3

TIL MY CASKET DROPS

RESTRAINING ORDER

RESTRAINING ORDER 2

IN LOVE WITH A CONVICT

Coming Soon

BONDED BY BLOOD 2

BOW DOWN TO MY GANGSTA

Royal Nicole